D1208636

THE YOUNG
SHAKESPEARE

The Young Shakespeare

ROSEMARY ANNE SISSON

Illustrated by
Denise Brown, R.E.

MAX PARRISH · LONDON
&
ROY PUBLISHERS INC. · NEW YORK

PUBLISHED IN GREAT BRITAIN BY
MAX PARRISH AND CO LTD GULF HOUSE PORTMAN STREET LONDON WI

PUBLISHED IN THE U.S.A. BY
ROY PUBLISHERS INC. 30 EAST 74TH STREET NEW YORK
N.Y. 10021

Fifth Impression 1965

To my Father,
who is responsible for
anything which is good in this book –
but for none of its errors –
and to my Mother who encouraged
me to write it.

Library of Congress Catalog Card Number: 60–6950

© ROSEMARY ANNE SISSON 1959
MADE AND PRINTED IN GREAT BRITAIN BY
PURNELL AND SONS LTD PAULTON (SOMERSET) AND LONDON

Contents

STRATFORD SONNET

Not like some peevish fugitive from death,
Disputing life's completeness with the tomb,
Nor, grossly garmented in all but breath,
Treading the boards of some frequented room —

No! Spirits do not show skull-dwindled faces,
Nor raise their melted eyelids out of sleep,
But gentleness still keeps familiar places,
And country memories are long and deep.

The swans, strong-beating in the evening air,
Call you, with us, to note their tuneful pride,
And doubled pleasure is it still to share
The kingcups, prodigal on Water-side.

Waking, with you we lie and listen still
To cuckoos calling up on Welcombe Hill.

R.A.S.

I

The Actors are Coming

'The actors are coming!' cried William. 'The actors are coming! The actors are coming!'

He said the words over and over again, his five-year-old voice as shrill and monotonous as the blackbird's which made its endless cry of 'chink, chink, chink' on the apple-tree behind the house on winter mornings. But now it was summer, and William stood quite still in the middle of the room and sang his own happy, lonely song, which he had repeated so often that now the words hardly had any meaning, even for himself. He had heard them first from his father, as they were finishing breakfast.

'Come here, my son,' said John Shakespeare, 'I have some news which will please you.'

'Wait!' exclaimed William's mother, as he began to scramble down from his stool. 'Finish your milk first! Husband, don't you know better than to interrupt the child at his breakfast? William, you've left a crust of bread there. Eat it up at once.'

'But it's burnt, Mother.'

'Burnt? Nonsense!' cried Mary Shakespeare. 'The bread I make is never burnt. And if it is,' she added, looking at it more closely, 'now that there is butter on it, you must certainly eat it. Waste not, want not.'

It was a curious thing about William's mother that it always seemed to worry her when good things happened to her family. If they were given fine birthday presents, she told them not to expect so much again. If someone praised their looks, she said, 'Handsome is as handsome does.' And when by chance one of them did something really clever, she always said, 'Don't let it make you proud.' It was as though she wanted to make sure that something sour should always be mixed with the sweet, just as every year on the first day of spring, she made a bitter-tasting medicine of herbs and dosed them with it.

So, now, she frowned as William, gazing anxiously at his father over the rim of his cup of milk, choked on the crust of bread (it *was* burnt!), and even when he had finished, she scolded him for wiping his mouth with his hand instead of using his napkin.

'There is no hurry,' said John Shakespeare, much amused. 'The news will wait. Now,' glancing at his wife with a twinkle, 'has the child finished his breakfast?'

'Wipe your mouth carefully, William,' said Mary Shakespeare. 'Fold your napkin. Now, get down from your stool – don't kick the legs, child! Put it over in its place, against the wall. Now, go and wash your hands—'

'No, no!' cried William's father. 'The news has waited, and so have I, quite long enough. William shall wash his hands afterwards.'

'Well—' said Mary, doubtfully. 'You spoil the child.'

But she sat and watched as William ran to climb on his father's knee and hear the news.

'A Company of Actors is coming to Stratford today,' said his father. 'There is to be a dinner, and afterwards they are to perform a play in the Council Chamber. Since you are the Bailiff's son, you are to be allowed to come to the play.'

William thought it over. He really knew nothing at all about actors. On the other hand—

'Can I come to dinner as well?'

'God bless the boy!' cried his father, laughing. 'Does he care more for his dinner than for a play?'

But his mother frowned again.

'A little boy go to dinner with the Council!' she said. 'No, certainly not. Whatever next! William, you think too much of food.'

'Well, well,' said his father, 'it is natural in children. But remember, Will, there will be many dinners, but the actors will not come to Stratford every day – especially these actors. They are the Queen's Interluders. There, my boy, now I must go to the shop. Be a good child and help your mother, and after you have had your dinner at home, she will bring you to see the play.'

He lifted William down.

'And remember,' he said, smiling, 'to hold your tongue while the actors are speaking. They have their own play. They don't want you to write another one for them!'

He strode off to his workshop, leaving William bewildered but excited. He hardly noticed the bustle about him, as Margery, the maid, lifted his young brother, Gilbert, down from his stool, washing his face and hands, and setting him to play in the corner. Then she cleared away the breakfast, wiping the trestle table and moving it to its place standing up against the wall. When that was done, she began to sweep the floor, sprinkling water to lay the dust. Her strong, capable hands kept moving William from place to place, as he stood in the way of her broom, but his mind was still busy with the unfamiliar and exciting event. 'The actors are coming.'

His mother had gone upstairs to feed the baby, and presently William followed her. On her lap, his fat little sister kicked and crowed, glad to be free from the swaddling-bands in which she had been wrapped all night.

'Mother,' he said, 'will the Queen be in the play today?'

'The *Queen*?' cried his mother, scandalised. 'The Queen, play with a parcel of rascally actors? Whatever gave you that idea?'

'Well,' said William, 'Father said they were the Queen's – the Queen's—'

'The Queen's Interluders', said his mother. 'Ah yes, that may be. Pass me the baby's smock, Will. Now the petti-coat. Yes, it may be that Her Majesty allows the actors to play before her, and pays them some money each year, and lets them wear her livery—'

'What's a livery?' asked William.

'A coat made of red cloth, which shows them to be the Queen's men.'

'*I'd* like to be a Queen's man,' said William.

'But as for *playing* with them – Her Majesty has some-thing better to do. She is busy ruling England. Pass me the baby's cap. And now her bib.'

William brought them to her, and then leant over the baby.

'The actors are coming, Joanne,' he said. 'The actors are coming.'

He loved his little sister, who always laughed when he played games with her, and seemed to enjoy his company far more than his brother Gilbert did. But now the baby was hungry, and pushed him away and began to cry.

'William!' exclaimed his mother. 'Don't tease your little sister. Go downstairs and tell Margery to heat the baby's pap, and to bring it to me here, with the silver spoon. And tell her not to make it too hot as she did yesterday. And William—!' she called, as he set off, 'go and play with your brother and keep him amused. I am too busy this morning to have you under my feet!'

William delivered his message to Margery, who, with

her sister, Audrey, was washing the breakfast dishes. Then he wandered back into the living-room, and sighed. It was just as he had thought. Gilbert, even at three years old, was perfectly well able to amuse himself, and didn't in the least want anyone else to help him. At the moment, he was fishing. He had a stick, and tied to the end of it was a piece of thread from his father's workshop, and he was sitting perfectly still on a stool, dangling the thread to the floor.

'Gilbert,' said William, 'the actors are coming.'

Gilbert looked at him, and thought it over.

'What will they do?' he enquired.

Now that, of course, was exactly what William didn't know, but he wasn't going to say so. He waved a vague hand.

'Oh, they wear red coats,' he said, 'and they – they play.'

'*I'm* fishing,' said Gilbert, making it plain that he was far more interested in that than in the actors.

He drew up the line, took an imaginary fish off the imaginary hook, put it in his cap which lay on the floor beside the stool, baited the line with an imaginary worm, threw it back again, and sat motionless once more. William began to feel that his presence was unnecessary – which was the usual fate of anyone who tried to amuse Gilbert.

Margery came through from the kitchen, carrying the little dish of bread-and-milk, and the silver spoon which had been given to Mary Shakespeare by her godparents when she was a child.

'Margery,' cried William, hurrying towards her, 'the actors are coming.'

'Fancy that now,' said good-tempered Margery, pausing at the foot of the stairs.

'And my father is the greatest man in the town, and so I am to see the play.'

'Margery!' called Mary Shakespeare from upstairs. 'Don't stand there gossiping! Bring the baby's dish up here!' and Margery hurried away.

William sighed again. What was the good of having a father who was the greatest man in the town – probably in the world, too – and of being allowed to go and see the actors, if there was no one to tell about it?

The sound of the blacksmith's hammer, singing clear in the morning air, gave William an idea. He waited until Margery was safely back in the kitchen, and then he slipped out into Henley Street. He went very quickly past his father's shop, seeing the apprentices sitting inside, stitching gloves, and his father talking to a customer. Next door was the shop of Master Wedgewood, who was a tailor and a friend of William's.

He was a little man, and seemed to William very old. He sat in his doorway working, with his spectacles on the very tip of his nose. (He had bought them from a pedlar, and they didn't fit him very well.)

'Well, neighbour,' he said, and threw William one quick, sharp glance over the top of his spectacles, poking them back onto the bridge of his nose, and bending over his work so that they slid down again. 'What is the news?'

'The actors are coming,' said William, solemnly.

'So I hear, so I hear,' said Master Wedgewood. 'I wish I could go and see them, but I have this suit which must be ready for a gentleman who is going off to London to-morrow. Isn't it a beautiful suit? I am just finishing the sleeves. Come closer, and you shall see it.'

But for once William could not spare a thought for the rich velvet and embroidery which was to make the gentleman look so fine in London, and which usually delighted him so much.

'Master Wedgewood,' he said, coming closer, but looking shyly down on the ground, 'Master Wedgewood, what do actors *do*?'

The old tailor took off his spectacles and rested his needle in his lap.

'Why they act plays,' he said, 'and sing, and dance, and tumble on the ground, and make people laugh.'

'Have you seen them, Master Wedgewood?' asked William.

The tailor coughed.

'Well, not exactly *seen* them,' he said. 'Not to say exactly *seen* them. You see, in my trade, the daylight is all. You cannot make small stitches by candlelight. And when the actors come to play, it is always the afternoon, and there is always some suit that a gentleman needs, or a petticoat for a lady, or smocks to be made, or a fine gown to be finished. But one day,' he said, 'one day when I am not so busy — or when they act a play in the evening by candlelight instead — then I shall go and see them.'

'*I* am going to see them today,' said William.

The tailor looked at him, and smiled, his kind old face crinkling up like a russet apple, kept all winter, and wrinkled now, but sound and sweet as ever inside.

'Then to-morrow you shall tell me all about it,' he said, 'and then I shall think that I have been there too.'

He put his spectacles on, and set to work again, and William turned away, feeling more satisfied. From the blacksmith's shop next door came a shower of sparks as the boy blew the bellows and the fire roared upwards. William paused, trying to decide whether or not to tell his news there as well.

The truth was that he found Master Hornby, the blacksmith, rather frightening. He was such a very big man, to begin with. And then, it was very hot inside the smithy, with the huge furnace and the steaming iron, so that

Master Hornby, swinging his great hammer, wore only a pair of breeches and a leather apron. Standing there, glowing red in the light of the fire and scowling at the horse-shoe he was hammering, he always looked to William just like the pictures of devils in the book which his father read to them all on Sundays. In those pictures, the good people were drawn up to heaven by angels, and the bad people were pulled down to hell by devils. The angels didn't look like anyone William knew, but the devils looked exactly like Master Hornby, and to have him almost as a next door neighbour was rather disconcerting. But perhaps, thought William, even a large and alarming blacksmith would be interested to hear that the actors were coming, and that he, William Shakespeare, was going to see them.

However, just as he was moving rather uncertainly towards the open door of the smithy, he heard his name called in a shrill voice. He looked back and saw Audrey waving at him. Audrey was quite different from her sister, Margery. She had yellow hair which was always flying into her eyes, and she giggled a great deal and forgot everything she was told, and dropped things. Mary Shakespeare only kept her as her second maidservant because she was Margery's sister, and often said in exasperation that she would rather have Margery a little less sensible, if only Audrey could be not quite so silly.

'William!' cried Audrey, now, running towards him. 'Master William! Oh, you naughty boy! What are you doing out there?' She took him by the hand, and began to drag him back towards the house. 'Don't you know better,' she said, 'than to go near the blacksmith's? Don't you know that every blacksmith is a son of the devil? Do you want him to catch you and throw you into his fire?'

'No,' replied William, with perfect truth, trotting along at her side. 'No, I don't!'

'You come inside at once,' said Audrey. 'Your mother is very angry with you!'

Mary Shakespeare was waiting for them inside the door and at once William forgot even the terrors of the blacksmith's fire.

'William,' said his mother, 'I told you to stay here and amuse your brother, and you disobeyed me, didn't you?'

'Yes, Mother,' said William.

He knew that it was no good trying to explain about Gilbert's fishing, or about the news which he had felt must be told to someone.

'You don't deserve to go to the play,' said his mother.

William remained perfectly still, gazing up at his mother without a word. Nothing in the world mattered to him at that moment but that he should be allowed to go and see the actors. He stood and waited, holding his breath, while a cart rumbled by in the street outside, and the baby murmured and laughed in her cradle in the corner of the room.

'Well,' said his mother at last, 'your father has arranged for you to go, and I don't want him to be put to trouble for nothing. You can go, but mind you stay here in this room and keep out of mischief for the rest of the morning.'

'Yes, Mother,' said William.

So here he was now, with Gilbert still catching imaginary fish, and the baby sucking its coral, and his mother and the two maids stepping to and fro between the kitchen and the storeroom, while he, young William, amidst the bustle of the Stratford household, sang to himself a song he hardly understood and waited for the beginning of the great adventure.

2

Going to the Play

It was dinner-time at last. William's father had changed his gown and gone off to the Council Chamber, and the two apprentices came in from the shop. Since their master was not at home, there was no meat dish, but only pottage, a thick soup with oatmeal in it, and bread. (What William wanted at the moment more than anything else – except, of course, going to the play! – was to have his own knife and to be allowed to cut up his own bread and meat with it at table, as the grown-ups did.) A dish of fruit, with beer for the maids and apprentices, and water for the children, and the meal was over.

Then, of course, William had to be washed once more, have his hair combed, and be dressed in his best clothes, until at last it was time to set out for the Council Chamber.

He felt very proud of his mother as he hurried along at her side, taking two or three steps to her one firm stride. She was wearing her best russet gown and hood, and round her neck was a snowy-white ruff, and the gold chain his father had given her for a New Year's gift. Best of all were her gloves, which his father had made specially for her, and which were perfumed, just like those worn by the ladies at Court. Mary Shakespeare often said that fine clothes were a foolish vanity, but when she was dressed for a special occasion, no one ever looked as handsome as she did, with her dark hair and hazel eyes, and that proud way of holding her head, as though to be the daughter of an English gentleman and the wife of an English tradesman was the highest honour in the world.

William wished that he himself could have been wearing a doublet and hose, as some boys of his age did, but instead he was still wearing skirts, just like a little boy – just like Gilbert. He knew better than to mention it to his mother, however, even if he had not been too much out of breath from excitement and hurrying to do any such thing.

'Are we – the only people in Stratford – to see the actors?' he gasped, as they turned the corner into High Street.

'No,' his mother answered. 'They are going to give a public performance later. But first they are to show the play to the Council and their wives.'

'And – to – me,' said William, jerkily but blissfully.

His mother glanced down at him.

'Don't let it make you proud,' she said, but this time her eyes were gleaming with an amusement which William immediately recognized. Usually, his mother was too busy, and too much occupied in being firm and improving, to be able to laugh with him, and for a moment it was as though there was some gay secret between them, as he smiled up at her his gap-toothed smile, and she smiled back. Then they had arrived at the corner of Chapel Lane, and she stopped to straighten his dress, and pulled his cap off to tidy his hair and put it on again rather less comfortably than before, and told him to be quiet unless he was spoken to. The next minute they were in the large, oak-lined Council Chamber.

The Councillors had finished their dinner, and the tables were already being cleared away. The room was full of noise, laughter and loud voices. As his mother stopped to speak to some people inside the door, William, jostled and towered over, felt like a very small mouse in a tall and boisterous cornfield. He didn't dare to take hold of his mother's skirt, but stood close to her, looking up from under his cap (which she really had put much too far over his forehead) while the greetings and comments on the weather and jokes about the size of the dinner the Council had eaten and the wine they had drunk rolled and rumbled above him like thunder in the heavens.

It was a relief when someone did speak to him at last, even if it was only Master Quiney. Adrian Quiney was his father's best friend, and a well-meaning, kind-hearted man, but as far as William was concerned he had one dreadful fault. He always began every conversation with a question to which there was no answer. So now, he said in his rather piping voice, 'Well, young William, and what have you got to say for yourself?'

The only truthful reply at that particular moment would have been 'Nothing,' but William knew that even if it satisfied Master Quiney, it would never do for his mother. Instead, he said politely, 'God be with you, Master Quiney,' and felt he had done rather well, but even so, his mother, who had seemed to be deep in conversation, found time to nudge him sharply, and to say, 'William! Take your cap off and make your curtsey! Master Quiney will think you don't know how to behave!'

William did as he was told and blushed. A moment later, he caught sight of his father, and ran forward thankfully to join him.

Places were now being set out for everyone who was going to watch the play – mostly stools and benches, but with some chairs in the front – and at the other end of the room, where the dishes had been carried away behind the serving-screens, a space had been cleared. Here, men and boys were coming and going, setting out odd pieces of furniture, stools, a chest, and a table, while a rich piece of tapestry was flung over the screens. There seemed to William a great number of these men, but perhaps there were only two or three, hurrying in and out, stopping to speak to each other in low voices, and having a strange air of not knowing that there was anyone else in the room. One of them would come out with a pewter pot (rather battered) which he would put down on the table, and then he would stand back, as though to see that everything was in its right place, and another man would come out to join him, and they would exchange a few words, and then both of them would stand back and survey the furniture, and then they would move the table an inch or two, and then a third man would come and join them, and *he* would stand back with his head on one side, and all the time you felt that they were quite unconscious of the crowded Chamber, the Councillors and Aldermen and their wives, of the Bailiff, John Shakespeare, glancing at them as he talked to his friends, and of young William staring at them so intently. Nothing, it seemed, mattered to them except what they were doing.

Excitement was stirring inside William so strongly now that he did not know how to keep it quiet without jumping up and down, and that he knew he must not do. Instead, he compromised, wriggling his toes inside his shoes, and bouncing a little on his heels. Even so, in a moment his father's hand fell sharply on his shoulder to keep him still.

'Well, my child,' said one of the Councillors, when this happened, 'and do you want to see the play?'

'Oh, yes, sir!' cried William, and then they all laughed, though he could not think why they should.

'Ah, well,' said the Councillor, 'I can remember the time when *I* would have walked barefoot ten miles to see a play!'

'Yes,' said another, 'what it was to be young! It's different now. I would not have troubled to come today at all, but I felt it to be my duty.'

'Yes, and a tiresome duty it is,' said Master Quiney, who had joined the group. 'I do not care to leave my business in the middle of the day, I can tell you, and the apprentices idling their time away, no doubt, and eating me out of house and home.'

The other Councillors all agreed, but John Shakespeare looked smiling from one to the other, and then said in a firm, loud voice, 'Well, for my part, I enjoy a play. I always did and I daresay I always shall, and I don't care who knows it!'

And William, who had begun to think that to become excited over actors was rather foolish, felt happy again, and began to bounce once more.

With a suddenness which made William jump, a trumpet sounded from behind the screens. It was rather a hoarse trumpet, and not unlike a cock crowing, but still William thought it was the most thrilling sound he had ever heard. There was a moment's silence, and then a new burst of noise and laughter as everyone began to find a place to sit. A stool had been placed for William between his mother and father, but his father took him on his knee, saying he might find the play too alarming.

When they were all settled, the trumpet sounded for the third time (more hoarsely than ever, like a cock who has just noticed a cat climbing up the roof of the hen-house) and a man came out from behind the screens, looked at them all with a confident smile, bowed and started to speak. The play had begun.

If you had asked William what it was all about, he could never have told you, either then or years afterwards. Truth to tell, a good deal of it consisted of long, long speeches,

of which he couldn't understand a word. But in between—! Oh, in between—! There was a man who played
the fife and danced as he did so. There was a man (the
same one) who turned six somersaults one after the other,
and then walked out on his hands. There was a Friar,
whose habit was tied up with a long piece of rope which he
kept getting between his legs and tripping over. And there
was a fight between three men (one of them was the Friar)
in which they fell over stools and rolled under the table,
and threw pots at each other (no wonder the pots looked
rather battered). William's father laughed heartily, and so
did his mother, though somewhat less heartily. The Councillor who said he had only come from a sense of duty
roared with laughter, and even Adrian Quiney could be
heard every so often saying 'Ha-ha! Ha-ha!' in a brisk,
business-like way. But as for William, he thought he had
never in his life seen anything so glorious, so hilarious, so
convulsively funny. It was fortunate that he wasn't sitting
on a stool, for several times he doubled up in an ecstasy
of mirth, and only his father's arm saved him from rolling
forward onto the floor. He knew that the Councillors
were laughing at him as much as at the play, and one of
the actors once or twice said something about 'The small
gentleman in the front row' which made them laugh more
than ever, but William didn't care, and even his mother
leaning across to tell him not to get too excited could only
check him for a moment or two. When the play ended at
last, he leaned limply against his father's shoulder, feeling
that life could have little more to offer, although when the
actors came forward to bow, he managed to rouse himself, and clapped harder than anyone else. Later, when
they had retired behind the screens his father sent for the
leader of the company. This was the slight, wiry man who
had done the dancing and tumbling, and his name was

John Smith. William gazed at him, fascinated, surprised to find how much older he looked now than when he had danced and laughed and tumbled in the play.

'Why, he is quite an old man,' he thought.

The actor, who had been answering John Shakespeare's questions, suddenly looked down at William. He had brown eyes which were very round and bright, and they moved quickly while he talked, as though at any moment he might fling out of the conversation into a backward somersault.

'Well, young sir,' he said, 'and did you enjoy the play?'

'Oh yes!' cried William. 'It was very funny. You were very good,' he added. 'You did your part very well.'

John Smith bowed to him, just as he had to the audience.

'Thank you,' he said, gravely.

He looked at William's father.

'He's a good, forward child,' he said, 'with a clear voice.'

'Too clear,' said William's father, laughing, 'and heard too often.'

The actor's eyes twinkled. He had a look of mischief, like a small, brown monkey.

'Perhaps you should have him trained as an actor,' he said, 'and make use of his voice.'

'No, no,' cried John Shakespeare, laughing, 'he is to become a glover, like his father, and make his fortune.'

'His fortune?' said the actor, and smiled. 'Yes, he will scarcely make his fortune as an actor. I know it too well. But a man must do what he must.' He looked down at William, still smiling. 'What do you say? Would you like to be an actor?'

William thought of the laughing and the clapping, and of that exciting moment when everyone watched one man, and he stood before them like a king.

'Oh, yes!' he cried. 'Oh, yes!'

Suddenly John Smith stopped smiling, and a strange look came into his face, a look which William didn't understand. Remembering it long afterwards, he thought that it was very sad, but at the time he only thought it was a strange look. The actor put a hand on his shoulder for a moment, and then, without saying any more, he bowed to William's mother and father, and turned away. William still stood and watched him while he spoke to other Councillors, and bowed, and smiled, and received from the Chamberlain the fee of four shillings for playing before the Council. John and Mary Shakespeare took leave of their friends, and drew William away, but though he still gazed backwards over his shoulder all the way out, John Smith never looked at him again.

They walked home in the summer evening, with William very silent now, half in a dream, and as they turned into Henley Street, his mother said indignantly, 'The impudence of the fellow! William become an actor, indeed! Whatever next?'

3

School

The next thing, in fact, was school. It was two years later that William lay awake in the bed he shared with Gilbert and thought about it with considerable excitement, but even more anxiety. From all he had heard from Richard Quiney, who had been there a year already, going to school was a very frightening business.

'We are beaten all the time,' Dick had said. 'Every boy who can't do a whole page of writing without a mistake is beaten.'

'But I can't write at all,' said William in great alarm.

Dick had come on a visit with his father, and the two boys were leaning against the hen-house in the garden, Dick very grown-up, with his own knife at his belt, and William in all the new-found glories of doublet and hose, but feeling young and inexperienced for all that. In spite of being a year younger, he had always before led, and Dick Quiney followed, but now Dick was suddenly knowledgeable and lordly.

'Oh well, you'll certainly be beaten. And we all have to make our own pens.'

'But I haven't a knife,' said William.

'The master will beat you for that, too,' said Dick.

William told these terrible tidings to his mother who was busy in the store room, cutting up apples to be dried for the winter, but she didn't seem to understand in the least how serious it was.

'If you're such a fool as to believe everything you're told,' she said unsympathetically, 'then you do deserve to be beaten.'

William lay and thought about all this in considerable agitation, very much regretting at this moment that his father's position as a burgess of the town entitled his son to go to the school, and wondering how he could ever have longed for this day to come.

He heard the maids stirring about in the room across the passage, and heard them go downstairs to light the fires. It was a chilly autumn morning, and the bed, with its stuffed woollen mattress and woollen blankets, was warm and safe. When Margery called to him from below, William snuggled closer and pretended to be asleep. But the next moment, his mother's voice called, 'William! Get up and dress yourself at once! It is nearly six o'clock. Do you want to be late, your first morning at school?'

William got shivering out of bed, feeling for his clothes in the half-light, and envying Gilbert who calmly lay and watched him.

'Here's your clean shirt,' said Margery, hurrying in. 'I have aired it at the fire. And here is a basin of water for you to wash your face and hands. I've warmed it a little – but don't tell your mother! Master Gilbert, you had better get up, too, if you want any breakfast, for everything is forward this morning, and your mother is dressed already.' And Margery set down the basin and hurried away.

'My garters!' wailed William. 'Margery, I can't find my garters!'

'I laid them ready for you with your stockings,' said

Margery, turning back. 'There they are! You have knocked them on the floor. Now, hurry, there's a good boy, or you will keep your father waiting.'

William, struggling with the points which tied his doublet and hose together, heard his mother go down the stairs, heavily, because she was carrying Joanne, as he could hear from the prattling voice which went with her. Joanne had learnt to talk early, and her father said she had never stopped since.

'I shall be late!' said William, despairingly, deeply regetting those extra minutes in bed. 'I shall be late, and the master will beat me!'

'No, he won't,' said Gilbert, now out of bed, and getting dressed in his usual neat, leisurely manner, 'because Father will be with you. I wish *I* was going to school.'

'I wish you were!' cried William, gathering up his cap, his mittens and his coat, and setting off for the door, dropping his cap and stooping to pick it up, then dropping one of his mittens and stooping for that. 'I wish you were going instead of me!'

'Are you ready?' said his father, as he came stumbling downstairs with his coat between his legs. 'That's a good boy. Where's Gilbert?'

'Here, Father,' answered Gilbert, miraculously dressed and washed, and perfectly calm.

'Good,' said John Shakespeare. 'Call the maids. Are we ready for prayers?'

They all knelt down, as they did every morning, and John Shakespeare said the morning prayers, with Joanne coming in each time particularly loudly on the 'Amen' because of having to keep so quiet in between. Then they turned towards the table for breakfast.

'What is that?' exclaimed William. 'There's something at my place. Is it for me?'

'You had better open it,' said his father, smiling, 'and see what it is.'

They all stood round to see him open the package, which was tied up with paper and thread, as though it was for one of his father's customers. Inside was a leather pen-case, and, in its own sheath, a knife with a bone handle.

'There!' said his mother, 'perhaps that will save you from one beating at least,' and she and his father both laughed, and William, looking from one to the other, found that some of the terrors of school were beginning to vanish.

After breakfast, there was a new bustle, as William struggled into his coat and searched for the mitten which had unaccountably vanished.

'Come, Will,' said his father, 'if you are to be a successful merchant, you must learn a little order and method.' That of course did nothing to find the mitten, but Gilbert went quietly upstairs and returned with it, saying, 'You must have dropped it when you picked up the other one which you dropped before.'

'Come here, Will,' said his mother, 'let me comb your hair.'

Usually she left this to Margery, but today she put her arm round him and drew him close to her knee, and combed the tangles out quite gently, and then she put his cap on and kissed him, almost as though she was saying goodbye to him.

'Come, then,' said his father, 'it's time to go. Oh, but wait, Will! There'll be books at school, and perhaps you will have to bring some of them home with you. Then there'll be the copies which you must make and your letters to learn. How will you carry it all?'

'I don't know, father,' said William, much distressed. 'Can't I carry it in my arms?'

'What, through the town?' said his father. 'That would never do. And then, you would be sure to drop something, wouldn't he, Gilbert?'

'Yes,' Gilbert answered firmly, 'he would.'

'What are we to do?' said his father.

William looked at him in dismay, and then caught sight of his mother's smile.

'Ah well,' said his father, reaching behind the chest, 'perhaps this will serve the turn.'

He brought out a satchel, beautifully made from one of his best skins, and hung it on William's shoulder.

'And don't lose it, Will,' said his mother, 'or let the other boys borrow it. Your father made that for you himself, and it's worth a lot of money.'

But William knew that no money could buy his mother's thought and his father's care, which sent him out of the house warmed and comforted for his first day at school.

It was still an alarming moment, though, as he and his father turned into the gateway in Chapel Street. The schoolroom was above the Council Chamber, and as they climbed the dark staircase he remembered longingly that day when he had come, carefree and excited, to see the actors play.

A number of boys were already in the schoolroom. Some of them were no older than William, but to him they were schoolboys, and so nearly as awe-inspiring as that figure in scholar's cap and gown who stood at the end of the room, with the birch-rods hung menacingly on the wall behind him.

'Good morning, Master Hunt,' said John Shakespeare, cheerfully. 'You see I have brought my boy to school. William, take off your cap and bow to your master.'

William did so, but after one hasty glance at the master's stern face and jutting nose, he kept his eyes on the floor.

'Is he a good child?' asked the master, in a deep voice. 'Is he apt to learn?'

'I'm afraid until now we have let him be idle,' said William's father. 'But I think he is quick enough – when he is not dreaming, and losing things, and letting his mind wander.'

'Don't, Father!' thought William in horror. 'Oh, don't say that!'

'I see,' said the schoolmaster. And then, rather more ominously, 'I see.'

'Well,' said William's father, 'I shall leave him in your hands, which I know are good hands.' He began to turn away. William looked up at him quickly in a desperate appeal.

'Be a good boy,' said his father, even more cheerfully than before, 'and study well.'

The next moment he was gone, leaving William alone with a roomful of strange boys and this tall, stern school-master.

'What is your name, my child?'

'William, sir.'

'Well, William, you must learn to make good use of the mind which God has given to you. To waste money is a great folly, but to waste your mind is a great sin. Do you understand me?'

'Yes, sir,' William answered, but rather dubiously.

'Do you know your letters? Can you write?'

'No, sir.'

'Then go to that place, there in the front, and take with you this board, which gives the letters of the alphabet. Take this straw, too. In a few moments, the Usher will come to you and as you point to each letter on the cross-row, he will tell you what it is. Then he will point with the straw, and you shall tell him. And then, I trust, you

will know them. Ask him to show you how to mend a
pen. Have you a knife?'

'Yes, sir,' said William, with a momentary flicker of
pride and hope, feeling that at last he had done well. 'And
a pen-case.'

'Very well,' said the master, not noticeably impressed.
'Go to your place, and after prayers you shall set to
work.'

William did work very diligently, assisted by the Usher,
a fresh-faced young man employed to look after the little
boys, or 'petits' as they were called, who could hardly
expect that a University man like Simon Hunt would
waste his time teaching them their A B C. William was
pleased to find how quickly he could learn the letters, and
he enjoyed copying them out on to paper with the quill
pen carefully prepared for him by the Usher, but even
so the morning passed very slowly, and when at last it
was eleven o'clock and they were dismissed for dinner,
he felt as though he had left home a year before, instead
of only a few hours.

When he arrived at Henley Street, they were all waiting
for him. His father had already come in from the shop,
and his mother had prepared a holiday dinner, with pottage, baked veal, a dish of artichokes, a salad, and a jelly,
set in her special party mould so that it looked like a red
rose. And for the first time, William was allowed half a
cup of his mother's home-brewed beer, instead of drinking
water like Gilbert and Joanne.

For once, too, when he talked, no one reminded him
that children should be seen and not heard, especially at
meals. With great zest, he described the morning's excite-
ments, how surprised the Usher had been because he nearly
knew his letters at only the second repetition, and how a
boy called Antony had received four strokes on the hand

with the birch rod because he hadn't learnt his lesson the night before, and because his only excuse was that he had been playing and had forgotten.

'If he was going to give an excuse at all,' remarked Gilbert, listening attentively, 'he might have made it a good one.'

'What?' exclaimed Mary Shakespeare. 'And make his fault worse with a lie?'

'Does being stupid make it better?' enquired Gilbert, and his father shouted with laughter and his mother couldn't for the moment think of an answer.

'Oh yes,' said William, 'and my pen was making blots and an older boy called Hamnet Sadler said he'd mend it for me, because the Usher was busy with another boy. And then Master Hunt said what were we talking about, and Hamnet said, "I am mending his pen for him," and then Master Hunt said, "That is good. But show William how to mend it, so that he may do it himself in future, and not trouble you." And Hamnet did show me,' finished William. 'He was very clever. He softened the end of the goose-quill by spitting on it.'

'Did he, indeed?' exclaimed Mary Shakespeare. 'I hope he didn't learn that trick from his father!'

Then John Shakespeare laughed again, for Hamnet Sadler's father was a baker.

Altogether, the dinner was a great success, and William liked to think that he had entertained them all with his stories. He went back to school quite cock-a-hoop – too cock-a-hoop, perhaps. That was really the trouble.

Afternoon school started quietly enough, and William settled down to copy out the capital letters, ignoring the drone of boys reciting Latin which went on all around him. He had managed the small letters quite easily, but the capitals in the English Secretary hand were full of the most intricate squiggles and scrolls, and much more difficult to copy and to remember. He discovered later that all the boys took pride in elaborating their handwriting tremendously, until each capital looked like the beginning of an illuminated manuscript, and he himself, when he learnt to join his letters up and to practise his signature, always decorated his 'W' with a special dot and brought the tail of his 'S' round in a fine careless swirl. But at the moment, he was having trouble enough following the Usher's meticulously simple copy.

He had just reached the 'H' – which was a particularly tricky one as you can see – when, with a dull 'spat!' a small, inky piece of paper landed right in the middle of his copy. William looked quickly around. All the boys were working hard, except for one red-headed boy, a year or two older than himself, who was sitting just behind William's left shoulder, and gazing fixedly out of the window.

William put his left hand over his eyes, and bent over his paper, but peeping through his fingers, he presently saw the red-headed boy tear off another corner of paper, dip it in the ink-pot, and flick it towards him, landing it this time on the floor by his shoes. William had carefully observed the technique of this interesting exercise, and as soon as the red-headed boy had turned back to the window, William tore off a corner of paper, screwed it up (he thought he wouldn't risk ink for the first time) put it against the point of his knife and flicked. He was all too successful. The paper ball went flying past the red-headed boy's nose and struck with considerable force against the cheek of the Usher, who was bending over the work of another boy just behind. The Usher straightened with an exclamation and William's head spun round towards the Master. A pair of icy grey eyes beneath fierce eyebrows were fixed directly upon him.

'William Shakespeare!' said the Master, in a terrible voice. 'Stand up!'

William did so, pulling off his cap, and feeling like a criminal who was just about to be hanged, and wondering if he could get a last message to his mother and father before it was too late.

'How *dare* you throw pieces of paper at the Usher?' exclaimed the Master. 'You are a naughty and ill-mannered little boy, and you deserve to be well beaten.'

The red-headed boy rose to his feet, and pulled off his cap, with the air of one politely entering an interesting debate.

'It was my fault, sir,' he said. 'And that was really meant to hit me. It was quite a good shot,' he added, apparently expecting the Master to be as gratified by this fact as he was himself.

'That is no commendation,' said Master Hunt, scowling horribly. 'It only means that William has been wasting all his time today in practising this idiot's occupation of flicking balls of paper about the room, instead of doing his work.'

'Oh no, sir!' cried William, horrified. 'That was the first time.'

'The first time!' said the red-headed boy, politely appreciative. 'Then it *was* a good shot, sir, wasn't it?'

The Master scowled more horribly than ever.

B

'Be silent!' he said. 'I shall not waste the other boys' time on your follies. You can both stay behind at the end of school.'

The rest of the afternoon passed miserably away for William. He thought of what his mother and father would say when they heard that he had been punished on his first day at school – and had deserved it, too. He wondered if he would be beaten, and looked with terror at the birch rod on the wall, and yet he thought that only to have to face the anger of this stern master was enough punishment in itself.

The time dragged by. William's pen began to splutter, and he did not dare to ask for help in mending it, but hacked the goose-quill about himself with his new knife, and then found that the ragged end left smears and inky scratches as he wrote. The light began to fail and the Usher brought in tallow candles which threw their flaring light unevenly over the books and paper, and made William's blotched and wandering capital letters assume strange shapes like dragons and weasels and porcupines.

At last it was five o'clock. The Master gave out the lessons which were to be prepared for the next day (William was to be perfect in all the letters on the cross-row) and then evening prayers were said.

'Good-night, boys,' said Master Hunt. 'Do not play the fool in the streets. Go straight home to your suppers, and learn your lessons well for tomorrow. God give you quiet rest.'

'Good-night, Master,' said the boys, all together, and went clattering out of the room and down the stairs, their voices rising in a sudden, rollicking roar outside the door.

'*Now,*' said the Master, to William and the red-headed boy, left standing alone in the suddenly silent room. 'Come here.'

They went up to stand before him, William apprehensive, and the red-headed boy with a polite air of interest in what was going forward.

'I will not have you wasting your time in class,' said the Master. 'Apart from the foolish disturbance that it makes, to allow you to be idle and naughty is to disappoint the wishes of your parents—'

The red-headed boy took a breath to speak.

'Or, of those who have the care of you,' added the Master, hastily. He bent his fierce eyebrows upon them, and William screwed his cap in his hands and thought with envy of the criminal about to be hanged. 'Next time it happens,' said Master Hunt, 'you shall be severely punished. However,' he said, with a very slight unbending of his frown, 'I do not wish to beat William Shakespeare on his first day at school, and so for this time he may go.'

'Thank you, sir,' said William, dismayed to find tears of relief in his eyes.

'You, William Hart,' continued the Master to the red-headed boy, 'are older and have more responsibility. I shall not beat you, but you will stay here and make copies for half an hour as a punishment.'

'Oh well, sir,' said William Hart cheerfully, 'that will come to the same thing, for my uncle will beat me if I am late home.'

There was a short silence, and then the Master, with a little, unexpected sigh, said, 'Very well. Perhaps that will make you more careful in future. Sit down and copy out this sentence on to a clean sheet of paper, until I tell you to stop. William Shakespeare, take your things and go home.'

William began to put his pens and paper and the tablet of letters into his satchel, but he felt very uneasy at the sight of the red-headed boy sitting working in the lonely room. William went to the door and turned, and hesitated.

'Sir,' he began, in a trembling voice.

'What?' said the Master, frowning.

'Sir,' said William, 'it doesn't seem right for me to go and for him to – for him not to.'

The Master scowled.

'You want to stay as well, do you?' he said.

William cast a despairing glance at the window, where the dusk seemed to press in upon the candlelit room, and he thought longingly of his family all waiting supper for him at home.

'No, sir,' he said, 'but—'

'But it offends your sense of justice, eh?' said the Master. 'That's a heavy burden to carry with you through life – a sense of justice.'

William did not understand him, but he stood by the door in acute discomfort and waited.

'William Hart,' said the Master, 'get your things together. You may go.'

'Oh. Thank you, sir,' said the red-headed boy, pleasantly surprised, but not visibly overwhelmed with gratitude.

He flung his tumbled possessions into a very ragged satchel, and set off to join William.

'And, Rufus,' said the Master, as he reached the door, 'do not expect me to be so easy another time.'

The red-headed boy suddenly smiled at him.

'No, sir,' he said, and led the way down the stairs.

'Why did he call you Rufus?' enquired William, as they reached the street.

'A lot of people do. I can't think why, can you?'

'No,' said William, puzzled. 'I can't.'

(It wasn't until about a year later that he had to translate the Latin word 'Rufus' and learnt that it meant 'red', and found Rufus grinning at him.)

'I'm glad the Master didn't keep us in school, aren't you?' said William.

'Oh, pooh, I don't care,' said Rufus.

'Wouldn't your mother and father mind if you were late?'

'They're both dead,' said Rufus. 'I live with my uncle. He might beat me for it, but he wouldn't really mind. No one cares what happens to me. That's the best of it. I can do what I like.'

He pulled his cap on to the back of his head, heaved his satchel higher on his shoulder, and turned away, saying casually 'Good-night. See you to-morrow.'

'Good-night,' said William, but he stood and watched for a few minutes as Rufus went jauntily off into the shadows of Scholars Lane.

It seemed to him that it might be a very lonely and frightening thing to have no one in the world to care what happened to you, and he realized how glad he was that he had a mother and father, and a brother and a sister, whose lives and thoughts were bound up with his own for as long as he lived. As the sound of Rufus' footsteps faded down Scholars Lane, he suddenly wanted to get home as quickly as he could, as though to make sure that they were all safely there and hadn't vanished during the afternoon. He began to run as fast as he could down the deserted High Street. He had never been out alone so late before, and he ran down the middle of the road, so as to avoid the piles of rubbish thrown in the gutters on each side. As he turned into Henley Street, he was nearly knocked down by a farmer on a heavy old horse, clip-clopping homewards through the town. He dodged, and saw the horse shy and heard the farmer exclaim angrily, but still he ran on, with his new satchel thumping at his side, until he was brought up short by the sight of the blacksmith's open door. Dusk had almost given way to darkness now, and the fire glowed terrifyingly, with the smith's huge shape towering beside it.

'He must be the Devil,' thought William. 'Oh dear! I'm sure he is the Devil.'

He tiptoed down the road until he was level with the glowing, spark-filled, hammer-thundering smithy, and then, clasping his satchel to him as though for protection, he ran like a mad thing for the shelter of his father's house, and arrived in the doorway gasping and panting.

He was safely past the smithy. But he still had to go back to school next day, and face the terrible Master Simon Hunt.

4

The Great Discovery

It was strange how quickly, after that first day, William became used to going to school. Of course, he was never ready in time. Every morning, Margery called him precisely at half-past-five, and every morning he dawdled dressing, or took too long over his breakfast, and had never packed his satchel the night before, and was always dashing out of the house in a panic, and running breathlessly through the streets, arriving outside the school just in time to see Rufus strolling up Scholars Lane. (This was not a reassuring sight; Rufus had never once been early.) As the clock struck seven, there William would be, pounding up the stairs and through the silent room to his seat, feeling the cold grey eyes of the Master upon him.

He sometimes thought that he would have come earlier if he had not been so much afraid of being late, and that it was the thought of Master Hunt's severe gaze which somehow made him dawdle and linger at home. It was the same with his lessons. He enjoyed learning, and was very quick to understand, but when he had to prepare a copy for the Master, or had to write a piece at his dictation, he always found himself in an anxious fluster, and his pen began to blot and his memory to fail, and when the work was given in, he would hear once more that stern voice saying, 'William Shakespeare, you can do better than this' – even though there were several others, older than he was, who had not done as well.

William soon made friends among the boys. There was always Dick Quiney, of course, arriving early, having prepared all his work, stodging away all day, and in the end getting no better marks than Rufus who idled half his time away. It seemed rather unfair, but somehow William enjoyed Rufus' company much more than Dick's.

'The trouble with Dick,' said Rufus, 'isn't that he's good, but that he makes everyone else want to be bad,' and William certainly found that the sight of Dick working away so diligently always made him long to do something simply dreadful—especially if he caught Rufus' eye a second later. He tried hard not to let Rufus lead him into mischief, after that first day, but he never could help being amused by him, and there were times when the whole school, including the Usher, would be laughing at something Rufus had said, except for Dick who had usually missed the point, and Master Hunt, who, William noticed, always scowled more horribly, the funnier Rufus was.

Another of William's friends was Tom Hornby, the blacksmith's son. It was, in a way, something of a disappointment to discover that Master Hornby was not the Devil at all, but a perfectly friendly and respectable smith, and William rather missed the excitement of his nightly dash past the smithy. But still, it was pleasant to hang over the half-door, chatting to Master Hornby, and on Saturday afternoons, his only free time from school, William several times spent a happy hour or two blowing the fire and learning how to shoe a horse. (His mother grumbled, though, because after this he always came home extremely dirty!)

But almost the best time of all was the moment when

school was over for the day, and they all lingered in the yard downstairs. They would stay there, breathing smokily, like dragons, in the frosty air, while the mist from the river whirled round the shafts of light from the schoolroom windows, talking and teasing each other, and being very witty, and inventing fearfully insulting names for their best friends, until the Usher would hurry downstairs, saying, 'Come, boys, off home with you, and don't dawdle on the way.' And then they would slowly disperse, shouting last messages down the road (just as though they were parting from each other for ten years instead of merely one night) until at last they had all gone their separate ways, with Rufus' voice always the last to be heard, shouting some brilliantly inventive insult from the shadows of Scholars Lane.

Christmas came and went, with its games and feasting, as well as long hours spent at Church, and visits from their cousins, the Henry Shakespeares from Snitterfield, and the Lamberts from Wilmcote. For the New Year, William made a special present for his father, a copy of the Lord's Prayer, written out in his own hand, with gold paint on the capital letters. Gilbert's New Year gift from his parents was a knife, like William's, and Joanne had a bunch of ribbons for her dress. William's present was a new pair of stockings, woollen, and very handsome.

Early in January, there was a great fall of snow, and, to the boys' amazement, Master Hunt gave them all a holiday, telling them that in such cold weather they would be better running and playing in the snow than sitting shivering indoors.

'I'll tell you what it is,' said Rufus, as they all went clattering joyfully downstairs, 'the Master wants to go sliding himself, and so he pretends to give us a holiday. Why do you suppose he told us to go up to Welcombe?

I'll bet if we went to Borden Hill instead, we'd find him there, sliding up and down all by himself on his flat cap!'

Whatever Master Hunt may have been doing, William and Rufus had a wonderful time, taking it in turns to go slithering down the icy slope on a piece of wood from the garden, and so did Joanne who had somehow wheedled them into taking her with them. In his careless way, Rufus was always very kind to the smaller children, and after that, Joanne often went with them on Saturday afternoons when they went walking by the river, or primrosing, or, later in the year, blackberrying. She would hurry along on her stumpy little legs, clutching at Rufus' hand, or getting under his feet, and in the evenings when she was tired and there was a long way to go, she would ride home on his shoulder.

So the year went quickly by, and in September they found quite suddenly that there was a new baby in the house. She was a very different sort of baby from Joanne, who, almost as soon as she was born, seemed to have a will of her own, and to laugh and kick and try to take her place in the family. This was a tiny little creature, very white and still, who cried in a thin, wailing way, quite different from Joanne's indignant yell. For many days, the house was kept very quiet, and the apothecary came several times and looked grave and shook his head, and the Minister came to the house to christen the baby, because they were afraid to take her out of doors. Even when the apothecary no longer paid his visits ('He is a useless fellow,' said Mary Shakespeare, 'and knows nothing!'), the little girl would often cry all night, while her mother or father or Margery walked up and down with her, and Joanne crept out of the bed she shared with the maids, saying, 'Let *me* take her. She always stops crying for *me*!' But gradually the baby grew a little stronger, until, in the strange way in which this always happens, she was no longer just 'the baby,' but a little person in the household, whom they loved all the more because she was so timid and delicate, and cried with strangers. She was christened Anne, but from the very beginning, they called her by the affectionate little name of 'Nan'.

Meanwhile, at school, William had left the English alphabet far behind. They spent an hour or two each week in music and singing, but otherwise it was Latin, Latin all the way. They began with Lyly's Latin grammar, taking it in turns to recite the parts of speech. Then would come translation of unseen passages, Latin into English, and then back into Latin again, sometimes verse and sometimes prose. Then, after dinner, came reading and translation of Latin authors, usually Cicero or Ovid or Virgil, and finally, when they were all getting very tired and the room had become hot and stuffy in summer or cold and airless in winter, came the thing William most disliked, construing the passage they had just read, and sorting out all its parts of speech, and reciting any irregular verbs which happened to appear in it.

'If these old fellows had had any consideration for us,' said Rufus, 'They wouldn't have written half so much. And if they *had* to write, at least they might have avoided irregular verbs.'

'I don't expect they knew they were irregular,' said William. 'I think they just had something they wanted to say, and they said it.'

'Then they should have been more careful,' said Rufus, severely. 'Besides, you don't tell me that talkative old fool, Virgil, didn't know what he was doing. "Of arms and the man I sing," indeed! Why couldn't he paint a picture instead? No harm in *that*!'

*

It was about this time that William made an interesting discovery. Among the books which his mother had brought from Grandfather Arden's house at Wilmcote were several books of poetry, and as soon as he could read, William fumbled his way through these, enjoying the stories of knights and ladies, and of Robin Hood and King Arthur. But he had never thought of poetry, of course, as something which was written by people one actually met. Poetry was found in books. Ordinary people, like the Shakespeares, wrote letters about business or signed the leases of houses, or made lists of household goods. And then one day, when William was struggling to translate the first line of a passage from Ovid's *Metamorphoses,* he found that the English words he was using fell into a sort of rhythm, like poetry. And then he found that he had a rhyme for the last word of the first line, and that the second line fell very easily into the same rhythm as the first. It was a rhyming couplet, just like the ones in his mother's books. Somehow or other, he went on, with only a little pushing about of the meaning here and there, until, before he knew what had happened, he had translated the whole passage into verse. He sat and looked at it in astonishment, and when he went to bed that night he lay and listened to Gilbert's breathing and he thought of that poetry, all his own, and he felt tremendously excited, as though something very important had just happened.

It was different, however, in the morning. When he first woke up, he had the feeling that there was something pleasant to remember, and he thought of his piece of poetry and laughed to himself, standing on one leg to put on his stocking. And then he thought of Master Hunt, and stopped laughing. What would he say when he saw what William had done? Among all the other boys' translations, properly written out in prose, as usual, he would suddenly come upon William's, nothing like the exercise which they had been set, but flying madly off into rhyming couplets. William imagined his fierce eyebrows darting up into his forehead, and his sharp voice saying, 'What is this? William Shakespeare, stand up! What is this? Where is your translation?' And when he found that William hadn't done a proper translation, but only written a poem instead, then he would be really angry. William wondered how he could not have thought of all this last night. Somehow, it had looked different then.

He hurried through his dressing, and the moment prayers were over, he gobbled his breakfast and managed to escape before his mother realized what he was doing. He ran all the way to school, arriving before anyone else, and sat in his place scribbling a literal translation of the passage as fast as he could. But first his pen had to be mended, and then the ink had gone thick and had to be watered, and then the boys interrupted him as they came banging in one after another, and long before he had finished, the Master arrived, and the Usher collected their work and handed it to him. In despair, William put the poem and his unfinished translation together, and bent the corners over, and handed them both in.

All the rest of the day, he wondered uneasily what the Master would say, and how angry he would be. When at last it was time for the work to be given back (for the Master always corrected it in the dinner-hour) he shrank into his seat and made himself as small as possible, and prayed. 'Please God,' he said, 'let him not notice that mine is any different from the others. Let him not notice that it rhymes.' But he hadn't much hope really. Not even God, he thought, could make his work look like Dick Quiney's, which was the only thing he wanted at that moment.

The Master frowned at the pile of papers in front of him, and his eye travelled slowly round the room and came to rest on William.

'William Shakespeare,' he said, fulfilling William's worst fears. 'Stand up.'

William stood up, and took off his cap.

'This translation into verse,' said Master Hunt, 'is this your own work, or did someone help you with it?'

'No, sir,' said William startled.

'You mean, someone did help you with it?'

'Oh, no, sir,' said William.

'You did it all yourself?'

'Yes, sir,' said William, and waited for the thunderbolt.

'H'm,' said the Master. He looked at it again. 'A little straining of the sense here and there,' he said, 'and one or two misplaced stresses, and one doubtful rhyme. But still, a pleasing venture. You have done well. Come here, and read it out to the school.' William, still incredulous, came and took the paper, glancing doubtfully up at the Master.

'Face the school,' said Master Hunt. 'Hold your head up. Speak clearly. Remember, poetry is the king who teaches language how to be most noble. Now, begin.'

William, in a glow of pride, confusion and astonishment, read his poem to the school, and as he went back to his place, he thought that he would never, in his whole life, be so happy again.

*

That was a most valuable discovery to William. To begin with, he used it carefully. He would first translate each passage, and make quite sure he understood it, and then let it fall into its English rhythm and rhyme. When he could not find a rhyme for the exact translation from the

Latin, then he would come as near to it as he could. But gradually, he began to use the poetry, not to translate the Latin, but to cover up the fact that he wasn't sure what the exact translation was. While all the other boys toiled away over the meaning of every word, he would get what he called to himself 'the general sense of it,' and then he would happily turn it into more or less rhyming couplets, or sometimes into blank verse, write it out in his neat, small handwriting and give it confidently to the Usher.

Now and then, Master Hunt would put a mark in the margin, or write something like, 'What is the exact meaning?' but that was all. William was delighted to have found in poetry such an easy way of avoiding work.

The Schoolroom, Stratford

5

Master Hunt is Angry

'Hey, Will!' called Rufus after school one day. 'Come down to the butts, and practise some archery.'

'I can't,' said William. 'I shall never get this translation done.'

'Oh, come on,' said Rufus. 'You can do that later. Just come for an hour.' And he added very solemnly, 'You know that with the Spaniards threatening the land, all able-bodied men should spend an hour every day training themselves in the handling of their weapons.'

'As though you'd spend an hour doing anything you didn't enjoy,' said William, laughing.

Rufus grinned.

'It's better than old Virgil, anyway,' he said.

They went down to the butts, on Water-side, and did some shooting at the targets. Their bows and arrows weren't new, of course. William had the bow his father had used when he was a boy (it was still rather large for William) and Rufus had borrowed one which Hamnet Sadler had grown out of. But John Shakespeare had taught them the proper movements of shooting, according to the rules – standing in the right way, putting the arrow to the string, drawing it the right distance, and then loosing it. He had even tried to teach them something about allowing for the strength and direction of the wind, but it must be admitted that the boys mostly just faced the mark, shot, and hoped for the best.

It was a fine evening and there were quite a lot of men and boys there, some shooting, and some watching and criticizing—because, of course, archery was something at which everyone felt he was an expert, even if he himself couldn't hit a church door at four paces. Suddenly, one man stopped shooting and called out, 'This is a dull business! Isn't there anyone here who will match me for a wager?'

Everyone stopped and looked at him. He was very tall, and he had a superb yew bow and a quiver-full of ash-wood arrows and quite obviously he was a former soldier, or else an archer by profession. There was a silence, and then a boy of about fourteen, who had been shooting at the next target, said, 'I'll shoot with you, if you like.'

'What for?' enquired the man, looking him up and down. 'Fruit candies?'

Everyone laughed, but the boy didn't seem to mind. He was sturdy-looking, with a round face and a country accent.

'No,' he said, 'for a shilling.'

'Oh well,' said the man, 'if you want to buy experience at the cost of a shilling, I don't mind. Six arrows, and the best three win.'

'No,' said the boy. 'Three arrows, and the nearest to the centre wins.'

The man shrugged his shoulders.

'Just as you please,' he said. 'The other would have given you a better chance.'

Everyone gathered round to watch as the two prepared to shoot, testing the strings of their bows and carefully choosing their arrows.

'Hoo!' said Rufus. 'I wish I had a shilling or two to wager. That man's a forester from over Alcester way. I've seen him here before.'

'Which would you bet on?' asked William.

'The man, of course,' answered Rufus.

'I'd wager on the boy,' said William.

'What?' exclaimed Rufus. 'You don't think he'll win, do you?'

'Well—' said William.

'*Do you?*' enquired Rufus.

'It would make a better story if he did,' said William.

A good many other people *were* laying wagers – mostly on the man, if they could find other people to take them, though one or two who had been watching the boy shoot were prepared to risk small sums on him. William was tremendously excited. It was like one of those contests in which the Unknown Knight challenges the famous Champion and defeats him. William felt that there should be a beautiful lady somewhere near to hang garlands round the neck of the winner.

The Forester shot first. As he notched his first arrow in the string, he glanced round and smiled, as if to say, 'This is hardly worth doing, but still—' He shot his three arrows very quickly, each steel-tipped and winged with goose-feathers. They sang through the golden evening air, the last one being shot before the first arrived, and stuck quivering in the target, while the bystanders clapped.

'Oh dear,' said William, as the boy stepped out, with his bow and three arrows.

'What did I tell you?' said Rufus. 'More fool him for putting himself forward. My uncle says if a man only does what he knows he can do—'

'He'd never do anything worth doing,' said William.

'Well, that's true, too,' said Rufus.

The boy shot very differently from the Forester. He took up his stance, and stood quite still staring at the target, and then notched his arrow, raised his bow, and very slowly drew it beside his cheek, and loosed the shaft. The first arrow was so wide that it almost missed the target altogether. There was a groan, and several men in the crowd who had laid money on him tried to say that they had only been joking. But the boy, taking no notice of the fuss, stolidly shot his second arrow, which fled beautifully straight and true to the target, with only one of the Forester's shafts between it and the centre. The crowd cheered, William danced up and down, and the friends of the men who had tried to withdraw their wagers now tried to agree. The boy took no more notice of his success than he had of his failure. There was a great hush as he shot this third arrow, and it was hardly loosed before everyone dashed after it. William and Rufus ran with the rest, but people were already turning back from the target as they arrived, and they could see the boy's arrow, its feathers very dingy beside the gleaming white ones on the Forester's, at least a quarter of an inch further from the centre.

William was bitterly disappointed, and he could hardly bear to look at the boy, who strolled casually up with the Forester, inspected the arrows, and then began to fumble in the purse which hung at his waist.

'You shot well, boy,' said the Forester. 'You can keep the shilling, if you like.'

'No,' said the boy. 'I always pay my debts. Here it is.'

He gave a shilling to the Forester, pulled his arrows out of the target and walked away. William and Rufus, following him, saw a girl of about sixteen come out of the crowd and join him.

'I'm sorry, Anne,' he called. 'I lost a shilling.'

The girl was very much like him, with a round face and grey eyes, and a serious look.

'Never mind,' she said. 'You'll win next time. Come on, we must hurry, or we'll be late for supper.'

He picked up his bow case and the rest of his arrows and they hurried away together.

'I wonder where they live,' said William, looking after them.

'Oh, Shottery, or somewhere out there, I suppose,' answered Rufus. 'They're not Stratford folk, I'm sure. Here, was that the clock striking? I'm going to be late for supper myself!'

'Supper!' exclaimed William returning from his dreams of defeated knights and of ladies consoling them with kind words. 'I haven't done my translation yet!'

'Take it up to bed with you,' Rufus advised. 'It's light until nine o'clock.'

'When are you going to do yours?'

'Oh, I did it during school,' answered Rufus carelessly, as they set off up Sheep Street. 'That was why I wasn't ready when old Beetle-brows told me to construe. If that bee hadn't stung you when it did, I was done for.'

'It didn't sting me,' said William.

'What?' cried Rufus. 'It didn't?'

'No. I saw it crawling on the table and I thought you needed some help.'

Rufus stood still, and solemnly held out his hand.

'I am your friend for evermore,' he said. 'Bid me do anything for you – except work of course – and I will do it. And if the actors in London know what's good for them,' he added, walking on again, 'they'll send a post-haste messenger begging you to join them. I never heard a man more fearfully stung by a bee in all my life. Why, there were even tears in your eyes. How did you manage it?'

'Oh, I just imagined how it would be if I was really stung by a bee,' said William. 'It was easy.'

*

It wasn't so easy, however, to smuggle pen, ink and paper upstairs after supper, and it was even more difficult to do the translation from Virgil when he got them there. However, somehow he scrambled some kind of poem out of what he took to be the sense of it, and scrawled it out by the fading light. He was by now so used to dashing off these translations in half an hour or so, that it wasn't until Master Hunt rested his hands on the pile of papers, fixed him with his cold eyes and said, 'William Shakespeare, stand up,' that he felt his first real qualm of anxiety.

'You have translated this passage into – ah – verse,' said Master Hunt.

'Yes, sir,' said William, fairly confidently.

'An exact translation, no doubt,' said Master Hunt.

'Er – yes, sir,' answered William, somewhat less confidently.

'Ah,' said the Master. He picked up William's paper. 'Where do you find this word, "stone"?' he enquired.

'It – it rhymes with "one",' William answered.

'*Does* it?' said the Master. 'Well, that is debatable. But where do you find it in the Latin original, which, though no doubt inferior, is the model for your own endeavours?'

'I don't know, sir,' replied William, his heart sinking.

Master Hunt returned to the paper.

'"Breeze",' he said. '"Breeze". Yes. It rhymes with "trees". You need not tell me that. But how is it that I am unable to find a corresponding word in the poem by Virgil of which, as you tell me, yours is an exact translation?'

'I don't know, sir,' faltered William.

'You don't know?'

'That is — because it isn't there, sir.'

'Just so,' said Master Hunt. 'It isn't there. We are beginning to arrive at the truth. Now, in the next line—'

So he took William through the whole passage, while
the school sat in frozen silence, and William grew hot
with shame. It seemed that the Master would never reach
the end, but at last he did, and looked at William for a
long moment. Then he very deliberately tore the piece of
paper across.

'That is a despicable piece of work,' he said. 'It is not
even a good poem in English.'

He let the two pieces of paper flutter to the floor.

'You will stay behind after school is over,' he said, 'and
do the task in a worthy manner. You may sit down.'

It was terrible to see the despised pieces of paper on
the floor for the rest of the afternoon, and when the
school was dismissed and William was left alone with the
Master, to see them still there, trampled and grimy. William had a strange feeling that he had just committed
some appalling crime and been discovered in it, instead
of merely having hurried over his homework, as Rufus
and half the other boys in the school did every night.

At last he had finished his translation, and took it up to
the desk. Master Hunt read it through.

'Yes,' he said. 'That is better.' He looked up at William.

'You think I am harsh with you, William,' he said.
William was horrified to find that his eyes were full of
tears and that he couldn't speak.

'Ah, Will!' cried the Master.

His face, with its jutting nose and fierce eyebrows was
suddenly not bleak at all, but very gentle.

'Why do you think I am angry when you are idle and

careless?' he said. 'My boy, it is because you have there in that great forehead of yours an imagination, and a keen intelligence, and the power to feel and understand. What does it matter if other boys flick pieces of paper about, and draw pictures of their Master, and leave the school as ignorant as when they came to it? But for you to waste those gifts of yours is an insult to them and to God who gave them to you.'

He reached out and touched William's head with his fingers. 'There is something in there, isn't there?' he said. 'Something which cannot be denied or forgotten. You feel it there too.'

'Yes, sir,' said William.

The Master smiled. It was the first time William had seen him smile, and he frowned at the same time, so that William suddenly wondered if he had always found Rufus funny after all, and had frowned because he wanted to smile.

'There,' said Master Hunt. 'Fetch me that vile thing there on the floor, and we will burn it together.'

William fetched the two crumpled, grimy fragments, and Master Hunt solemnly took out his tinder-box, and together they watched the two pieces of paper burn.

'In future,' said Master Hunt, 'honest prose or good verse, or a blank sheet of paper, but no more mongrels.'

'No, sir,' said William, and he actually laughed.

'Off you go,' said the Master, 'and join your friends. What is it to be? Shooting, or wrestling, or a game of All-Hid?'

'Shooting, sir,' said William.

'Be off with you, then.'

William gathered his things and went towards the door.

'And, William, when I next scold you, say to yourself, "My Master thinks I am worth being angry with".'

'Yes, sir,' said William.

He had arranged to go to the butts again with Rufus, but somehow he didn't. Instead he took the footpath up to Welcombe, and sat there on the stile, all alone. He sat looking down at the town below him, the thatched roofs and crooked chimneys, the winding river and the straight Church rising above it, and he thought of Master Hunt's words, and he felt, deep inside him, something like a great pain – somewhere deeper than his head, almost as if it was in the very middle of his body. He had never felt it before, and yet it was not entirely strange to him. It was as though he had felt twinges of it before at odd times, almost without knowing it, when he was running home in the evening, with the first stars in the sky, or when he woke up in the morning and smelt the green freshness of spring in the air, or when all the family were gathered for music after supper, singing together in the candlelight, his mother and father, Gilbert and Joanne and little Nan, and he himself watching them and listening to the music, and for a moment outside it all, and yet at the same time intensely part of it. Now it seemed that all these moments came together in this one strange, hidden longing, like being very hungry for something, and yet almost too excited to eat. He sat on the stile all alone for a long time, and he knew that there was something he must do, and a path which he must take – but what path it was, or when he should take it, or where it led, he did not know.

6

The Travelling Company

One Saturday morning, William rushed home from school in a state of great excitement. 'Mother! Mother! where are you?' he called, clomping into the house in his new, large shoes. ('They're nearly as big as your father's!' cried his mother when she bought them, seeing with horror how fast he was growing out of all his clothes.)

His mother answered him now from the chest by the window where she was sitting doing her household accounts, and she spoke severely, as she often did these days.

'What are you thinking of, William,' she said, 'banging into the house like that? Come in quietly, see where I am, and then wait until I am ready to attend to you.'

'Yes, Mother,' said William, checked, but still impatient. He came closer, and stood waiting while she wrote. Most of the boys' mothers could not read or write. At the most, they could sign their names, and usually they could only make their mark. But Grandfather Arden, having seven daughters and no sons, had been determined that his girls should be able to read and write and figure, and Mary Shakespeare had always been very glad of it.

'Two yards of holland to make smocks for Nan,' she was writing, '2s. 4d'. And then, 'Two pairs of stockings for Will and Gilbert, 2s. 6d. A pair of shoes for Will, 1s.

A petticoat for Joanne, 1s.' She put down her pen, and looked at what she had written.

'Everything seems to get dearer,' she said. 'Nothing is ever cheaper. And Richard is such a big boy that none of Nan's dresses will fit him.' For William now had a second brother, Richard, a cheerful, fair-haired little boy, very much like their father.

'There's no hope of handing on any of Joanne's dresses,' said Mary Shakespeare. 'She wears them into rags before I can even pass them on to Nan. I suppose I must try to get my shoes mended, instead of buying a new pair. That will save one and six – and then if I buy some stuff for Richard now, perhaps he can make it do until he has grown into the doublet and hose I laid aside from Gilbert. Thank heaven, *he* leaves his clothes as good as new. As for Joanne, she will have to have one of my dresses cut down. There is nothing else I can do.'

It seemed very strange to William that his mother should say all this to him. It was almost as if she was asking his advice, or wanted his help. He felt uneasy and impatient, for, after all, this was nothing to do with *him*. He had more important things to think of. He fidgeted a little, and his mother closed her account book, and sighed, and then looked up at him.

'Well,' she said, 'what did you want?'

William had for a moment an uncomfortable feeling that he had disappointed her, but he soon forgot it.

'Mother,' he said, 'may I go and see the actors?'

'The actors?' said his mother.

'Yes, at the inn. The Master allowed us to leave school early, so that we could go and see the play. May I go, Mother?'

'William,' said his mother, 'it is time you began to think of other things than just amusing yourself. You will soon have to start earning your own living. You won't be able to rush off all the time to see plays when you are working in a trade.'

William scuffled his feet. He couldn't imagine why his mother should talk about that now. He was still at school, and after that there was probably the University to come. And anyway, at the moment, all he could think of was the play.

'Stand up properly, William!' said his mother. 'Don't shuffle your feet like that!' She sighed again. 'Very well,' she said, 'you may go. What time does it start? I suppose you'd like something to eat now?'

'Oh yes, please, Mother!' said William, delighted.

'I'll tell Margery to bring you some bread and pottage,' said his mother, getting up. She paused on her way to the kitchen, and looked back. 'Do you have to pay to go in?' she asked.

'Yes, Mother, but not much. Rufus says we can stand in the yard for threepence.'

'Rufus!' exclaimed his mother. 'Are we expected to pay for him as well?'

'Oh no, he was given threepence for holding a gentleman's horse yesterday. I'll just ask Father for threepence for me.'

'No, wait!' said his mother. 'Don't—' she hesitated – 'Don't bother him with that now.' She felt in the purse which hung from her waist. 'Here,' she said, 'you can have threepence today. But don't always expect money to come from nowhere for your pleasures.'

'No, Mother,' said William, but he felt puzzled. He expected money to come from his father, of course, and from his father's business, as it always had.

'I wish you'd take me to see the play, Will,' said Joanne, who for once had kept quiet, and was sitting at the other end of the room with her sewing, while little Nan, beside her, practised sample stitches on a square of canvas.

'Mother would never let you go,' William answered.

'I know. Because I'm a girl,' said Joanne looking resentfully at the smock she was hemming. 'When I'm grown up, I shall go to plays all the time.'

'No, you won't,' said William teasingly. 'You'll be married, and you'll have to stay at home, and keep house for your husband. Women aren't allowed to do anything else.'

'All right,' cried Joanne, 'perhaps I won't get married! I'll cut my hair off, and put on boy's clothes, and go out to seek my fortune!'

'Your fortune,' said Gilbert, coming in at that moment, 'would be to be found out and sent straight home again. They'd know at once that you weren't a man, because you talk so much.'

'Yes, and I talk sense too,' Joanne agreed instantly, changing her ground. 'That would show that I was a woman!'

William laughed and Gilbert, defeated for once, grinned at him.

'Oh, Nan!' cried Joanne. 'Wait a minute. You're doing that wrong. Let me show you.'

'Fancy you teaching Nan sewing,' said Gilbert. 'Talk about the blind leading the blind.'

'Joanne teaches very well,' said little Nan, in her gentle way. 'Only sometimes, when she shows me, she stitches the canvas to my dress, and then we have to start all over again.'

The boys both laughed at that, and Joanne said cheerfully, 'Oh well, I notice you boys don't mind wearing the shirts I hem for you.'

'No,' said Gilbert, 'they're fine.' Joanne looked slightly

surprised, until he added, 'The stitches are so large that everyone thinks they're embroidered, instead of merely hemmed. If we wore the tail of the shirt outside our breeches—'

'Everyone would think you were an ass, and they'd be right!' cried Joanne, and returned, flushed, to her sewing, while Gilbert, satisfied to have annoyed her at last, smiled to himself, and picked up his book.

'Do you want to see the play, Gilbert?' asked William. 'You can come with us if you like.'

'No, thank you,' answered Gilbert calmly, sitting down by the window, 'I prefer to read plays, rather than to see them. They say actors always rant and rage on the stage, and spoil them.'

'But you've never seen a play!' exclaimed William.

'No,' said Gilbert. 'I would rather act them in my own head,' and he turned a page and vanished into his own private world, where no one ever followed him.

*

William met Rufus on the corner of the High Street.

'Where's Dick?' he called.

'His father wouldn't let him come.'

'Why not?'

'Said an inn yard was no place for his son to spend the afternoon, and that he would only meet a lot of disreputable fellows there.'

'Like us,' William suggested cheerfully.

'That's right,' said Rufus.

They turned and began to walk up Wood Street.

'Was Dick very disappointed?' asked William.

'I didn't see him,' Rufus answered. 'I just went into the shop and Adrian Quiney pounced on me and said Dick wasn't coming. Oh yes, and he said that if he didn't take care, I should make Dick as idle as myself. What do you think of that?'

'Ridiculous!' said William. 'No one could be as idle as you are!'

'That's what I told Master Quiney!' said Rufus, and they both shouted with laughter and went happily on together, arm in arm.

The inn yard was certainly very crowded, and some of the people there *did* look rather disreputable. William wasn't at all sure that his mother would have let him come alone with Rufus, if she had not been so obviously thinking of something else. There were a few gentlemen in the galleries, and quite a number of Council members and shop-keepers with their wives. William looked for Master Wedgewood, his old friend, the little tailor, who had sold his shop in Henley Street and gone to live with his married daughter, but he couldn't see him there. In the yard were mostly apprentices and schoolboys, with a number of country people, but a handful of rough-looking youths were there, too, who looked more like labourers from the smelting-works at Birmingham, or from the tanneries at Coventry, and whose loud shouts and laughter made the respectable local people look at them anxiously, and move away. However, since there was room not far from these youths, William and Rufus took up their places there.

'Have you any money?' asked Rufus.

'No, not a penny,' William answered, and he thought again how strange it was that his mother should have talked as though his father was a poor man, when he had a prosperous business, and owned three houses in Stratford, apart from the Arden inheritance at Wilmcote and Snitterfield.

'Well, I'll surprise you,' said Rufus, and produced a threepenny bit. 'My uncle gave it to me.'

'Your *uncle*?' exclaimed William in amazement, for Rufus often said that his uncle would as soon cut off his own head and throw it in the river as give away a half-penny. 'Whatever did he do that for?'

'Oh – well,' said Rufus, and hesitated. 'I'll tell you later. Anyway, I'm going to buy some apples and nuts.'

'I'm not really hungry,' said William.

'Nor am I,' said Rufus, 'but we must have some apple-cores and nut-shells to throw at the players if they're no good.'

He was just setting off, when there was a disturbance nearby, and they saw a girl being jostled by the crowd of youths.

'Come on,' said one of them. 'Come and stand with us. We'll look after you.'

'No,' she said, pushing him away. 'Go away. Leave me alone.'

'Now, now,' said another. 'That's no way to talk. A pretty girl like you shouldn't come to the play alone. You might get frightened.'

'I'm not alone!' she cried. 'My brother's here. Oh, go away!'

'I'll be your brother,' said the first one, trying to put his arm round her waist.

'It's the girl we saw at the shooting,' said William. 'I wonder where her brother is.'

'Oh, go away! Go away!' said the girl, almost crying.

'We must do something,' said William.

'What, us?' cried Rufus. 'Interfere with those great bullies? They'd eat us for dinner!'

'I don't believe you've got a brother,' said one of the youths.

'Oh yes, she has!' said William, and he began to elbow his way towards them.

'Here, wait a minute, Will!' exclaimed Rufus. 'You can't— They're much too— Oh, Lord help us!' he finished, and went after William.

'So there you are, Anne!' called William, as he got near. 'I'd lost you!'

'Who d'you think you are?' said one of the youths, and looked him up and down. 'Her brother, are you? Well, we don't need you!'

Rufus arrived, breathless, and with a resigned look on his face, at William's side.

'You remember Rufus, don't you?' said William to the girl, ignoring the youths.

'Oh yes,' said Rufus. 'I'm sure she remembers me. Couldn't help it.'

The girl looked at them both in astonishment.

'No,' said another of the youths, 'and what's more, she doesn't want to. Shog off, the pair of you. Go and play shove-penny!'

'Guess whom I saw over there?' William went on. 'Cousin Charles.'

'And who's cousin Charles?' enquired the youth who still had an arm round the girl's waist. 'A comfit-maker?'

'No,' said William, looking at him for the first time. 'He's a famous wrestler.'

The youth suddenly took his hand away. William moved closer to his pretended sister, and Rufus followed him.

'Oh, *him*!' said Rufus, cheerfully. 'That great, big giant of a man! I never knew he was your cousin!'

'Our first cousin, isn't he, Anne?' said William, and went on hastily, because he was afraid she might deny it. 'He's feeling worried, though.'

'Oh, why's that?' asked Rufus.

'He hurt a man rather badly last week.'

There was a sort of yielding movement in the group of youths, as though each of them had taken a step backwards.

'Oh, bad luck,' said Rufus.

'Yes,' said William, 'it was, for the man. He broke his back. Charles was very sorry about it. He said he only threw him over his shoulder, but the man must have fallen awkwardly.'

There suddenly seemed to be more space about them, and the rather unpleasant tanner's smell grew less.

'Still,' said Rufus, thoughtfully, but raising his voice, 'your Cousin Charles is nearly seven feet tall. That was a long way for the other man to fall.'

They looked round, and found themselves alone with Anne, who gazed at them wide-eyed. William took his cap off, and said politely,

'Good afternoon, Mistress Anne.'

She was well dressed, but plainly, in the country style, wearing a worsted gown and a French hood, with only a white frill at her neck instead of a ruff, and with all her hair drawn back beneath a linen coif. William thought that she was very pretty. She was still looking frightened, though.

'How do you know my name?' she asked.

'We saw you once with your brother at the shooting,' William explained. 'Where is he?'

'He only went to buy some oranges,' she said, 'and then those men—'

'Well, don't worry,' said William, feeling very grown-up and protective, 'I'll stay here until he comes back.'

But she still looked troubled.

'Have you really a Cousin Charles?' she asked.

'No,' replied William, gravely. 'Have you?'

She looked more troubled than ever.

c

'Then it was all lies,' she said.

'Well, not *quite* all,' said William. 'There is a famous wrestler called Charles. My father told me about him. And he must be *somebody's* cousin.'

Anne looked doubtfully from him to Rufus, while they gazed solemnly back at her. Then she suddenly laughed.

'Well, he did me a great kindness today,' she said, 'and so did you.'

She told him that her brother's name was Bartholomew, and that her father was Richard Hathaway, though some people called him Richard Gardener, because in his young days he had worked as a gardener. But he had inherited some money, and now he was a farmer, and rented his land from the Earl of Warwick. She had four brothers and two sisters, and they lived in the house called 'Hewlands' in Shottery. By the time Rufus returned from spending his threepenny-bit, with Bartholomew, whom he had met in the jostling crowds round the fruit-vendors, it was nearly time for the play to begin, and they all felt as though they had known each other for years.

'I've never seen a play before,' said Anne. 'Father would never let us come. He said plays were the wicked invention of the Devil. But Bart had to fetch a piece of harness from the smith, and I had some shopping to do in the town, so we thought we could slip in here, and he'd never know. What happens in a play?'

'Well, it depends what sort of play it is,' said William, cracking a nut for her, and flicking the shell at a stout gentleman in the gallery, who turned round indignantly and shook his fist in quite the wrong direction. 'There are Latin tragedies by Seneca, which are full of blood and ghosts and murders, and there are Latin comedies by Plautus, with jolly servants cheating their masters and twins getting mistaken for each other. But in the last

English play I saw, everyone ran about and quarrelled and laughed and fell over, and a jester did back-somersaults and tumbled on the ground.'

'Oh,' said Anne, 'I should like that.'

*

The trumpets sounded three times – not a cracked old trumpet, crowing out of tune, but a fine, golden flourish. And then, as the fruit-vendors stopped shouting, and the gentlemen in the galleries and on the edge of the stage settled themselves on their stools and stopped fanning themselves with their feathered hats, there was a wonderfully sweet sound of violins, and some men came on the stage, looking wild and strange, and dressed in leaves. One of them had a bundle of sticks, which they all tried to break in two. Then, when they couldn't do it, they each took a stick out of the bundle, and broke it easily, and soon had broken up the whole bundle. Then they picked up the pieces, bowed to the audience, and went out, and the music stopped.

'*That* was a short play!' said Bartholomew, in strongly disapproving tones.

'No, no,' cried William. 'That was only the dumb-show. The play is yet to come.'

'Oh,' said Bartholomew, thinking of his entrance money, 'I'm glad to hear it.'

'What did it mean?' asked Anne.

'Why, I suppose that a family or a kingdom divided against itself is easily destroyed.'

'Well, they got that from Aesop's Fables,' said Rufus, getting an apple-core ready to throw. 'I've just been translating that one at school. They'll have to do better than that!'

But the players did do better. Before Rufus could throw

his apple-core, music sounded again, and on to the stage came the most beautiful woman they had ever seen. She had long, fair hair, and wore rich clothes, and had a golden crown on her head.

'A Queen!' cried Anne. 'Oh, look, it's a Queen!'

With her was a young man, also magnificently dressed, whom they soon found to be her son, a Prince. She looked at him for a few moments in silence very sadly, and then began to speak in a clear voice, full of sorrow. All the great crowd of people in the inn-yard and the galleries, and lounging against the doors, listened without moving so much as a finger, and it was as though her first words laid a spell upon William from which he was never to escape again, as long as he lived. For she spoke in blank verse, that very blank verse into which William had so often translated Virgil or Ovid, only this was English poetry, written first in English, and used to tell a story and to express the feelings of a Queen of ancient Britain.

Truth to tell, the play never was quite so good again as in those first few minutes, but still it was exciting enough. It was all about a king who divided his kingdom up between his two sons, and told how the two sons quarrelled, and the younger killed the elder, at which his mother (who loved the elder best) killed the younger son. There were exciting shows between each of the five acts, first with the music of cornets, then of flutes, then of oboes, and finally, with a thrilling show of armed men marching round and round the stage, and firing their muskets in the air, to the music of drums and flutes. This was to show the rebellion in which the King and Queen were killed, and the terrible civil war which followed it.

'There wasn't much to laugh at,' said Anne, when the play was over, and the actors had come forward to bow.

'No, not much of a play,' Rufus agreed. 'Nobody killed on the stage at all. No blood or ghosts or anything. Just a lot of talk.'

But William was remembering the words of the old Councillor at the very end, when he said that the kingdom would find peace at last.

> *For right will always live, and rise at length,*
> *But wrong can never take deep root to last.*

He thought that he would never forget them.

Anne and Bartholomew were anxious to get home to Shottery, before their father wondered what was delaying them, so they said goodbye to William and Rufus in the yard, Bartholomew arranging to see them again at the shooting, when he could get away from the farm.

'And do you still think that plays are wicked?' William asked Anne, teasingly.

She answered, exactly as his mother might have, 'No doubt plays are like anything else. They can be used for good or evil.'

'Well, this one has been good,' said William. 'We met you because of it.'

'And Cousin Charles,' said Anne, unexpectedly, and went quickly away with Bartholomew, while William looked after her, smiling, and hoped that they would meet again.

William and Rufus lingered in the yard, not wanting to admit that it was all over. The players had gone inside to change their clothes, and also, no doubt, to drink the ale which some of the gentlemen would have ordered for them. The wooden stage which had been set up at the end of the yard furthest from the archway, still stood there, bare and empty, and William and Rufus, half-curious and half-awed were just moving near to look at it, when a boy of about their own age, or a little younger, came out of the door at the back, carrying a mug of beer. He climbed up on to the stage, and sat down on the edge of it, swinging his leg negligently. He had rumpled fair hair and greenish eyes, and his teeth stuck out slightly.

'By the Lord Harry and all his halidomes,' said Rufus (it was his favourite oath), 'that's the Queen of Britain! Let's go and talk to him!'

Anne Hathaway's House

7

The Boy who Played the Queen

The boy had a very blithe and carefree air, sitting there
swinging his leg and drinking his beer. He looked less
like a boy, in fact, than like a rather small man of an
independent nature and no family ties. In spite of his
shabby doublet and darned hose (darned with different
coloured thread too!), his manner, as William and Rufus
came near, was very much that of a King granting
audience.

'You played the Queen, didn't you?' asked William.

'Yes,' said the boy. 'Did you like the play?' he enquired,
and yawned, as though to show that he did not really care
about the answer.

'Yes, very much,' said William.

The boy nodded, in condescending agreement. 'Not
bad, was it?' he said. 'Of course we're not like some
companies, who send a parcel of ragged vagabonds out into the provinces, and call them by their own title. No,
you've the whole London company here – well – nearly
all of it. We don't insult our patron by lending his name
to the rag-tag of players.'

'Who is your patron?' enquired Rufus sarcastically.
'Alexander the Great?'

'We've a very good play about Alexander the Great,'
said the boy, not at all disconcerted. 'No, don't you know

our patron?' he went on. 'We're the Earl of Leicester's Players – the best company in England.'

'How about France?' asked Rufus, refusing to be impressed.

'I saw the Queen's Players once,' said William.

'Queen's Players? There's no such company,' said the boy. 'I suppose we're nearest to being the Queen's Players. At least, we play at Court.'

'These were called the Queen's Interluders.'

'Oh, *them*!' said the boy, and tossed off the last of his beer. 'They used to be good once, but then they became so bad, they *had* to travel. The last I heard of them, there was only one of the original company left. The Jester, John Smith, I think it was.'

'Yes,' said William. And he added, loyally, 'He was very good.'

'He was the only one who was,' said the boy. 'I heard that he held the company together for a while, travelling round the country. They're broken up now, though.'

'What's happened to John Smith?' asked William, remembering the little man with the gay, monkey's face and the sad bright brown eyes, who had made him laugh so much.

'Dunno,' said the boy, carelessly. 'You know what actors are like.'

'No,' said Rufus. 'What are they like?'

'Oh, they come and go. They play with this company, and that company. And then the plague breaks out, and they have to travel, or the city closes the theatre, and they have to starve, or else their lord dies, and they're left without a patron. Actors come and go. You never know where they are from one day to the next.'

'That would suit me,' said Rufus.

The boy looked him up and down.

'Why don't you join the company, then? They're always needing boys. Richard Robinson's voice broke only last week, and now he can't play women any more.'

Rufus laughed.

'My voice is just breaking,' he said. 'I wish I *could* join, though. Do you travel all the time?'

'In the summer we do, mostly, when the Queen moves the Court to Windsor, especially if there's plague in London. But in the winter – ooh, that's the best!' He forgot to be casual and superior, and sat up and hugged his knees. 'Since James Burbadge built the Theater, we have our own place, and people come to see us, and have their own favourite players, and give them presents. A gentleman gave me three crowns one day, because he liked my playing! And then at Christmas time, we play at Court, and the Queen sees us play—'

'Does she give you presents, too?' enquired William.

'No,' said the boy. He shook his head, regretfully. 'No,' he said, 'she likes to get presents, but she doesn't often give them. Sometimes she sends a message, though, to say she's enjoyed the play, and its marvellous to see her there, all in gold and jewels, with diamonds in her hair. It's enough to make a man forget his part.'

'Or a boy?' enquired Rufus.

'I don't forget *my* part,' answered the boy, scornfully. 'That's why I'm one of the leading actors.'

'How much do you get paid?' asked William.

The boy hesitated.

'Well, I'm not exactly *paid*,' he said, 'because I'm still learning the trade. But they give me a few shillings now and then, when we've had a good day; and when I'm a man, I shall earn a good wage – oh, ten shillings a week, and more.' Then he rumpled his hair, and peered into his empty mug. 'That is,' he added, 'when the company has it. But the trouble is, when we have bad plays, and people don't come to see them, nobody gets paid.'

'H'm,' said Rufus, 'perhaps I won't become an actor after all.'

The boy looked up at him and smiled.

'If you're an actor, you're an actor,' he said, and for a moment William was reminded of John Smith, the little jester, and how he had looked as he said, 'A man must do what he must.'

Some men were coming and going now between the stage and the inn-door behind it, and presently two of them carried out a big basket, just like a laundry-basket, and set it down with a thump.

'Here, you, Augustine, you young imp!' called one of them. 'Where's your gown? How can we shut this basket until we have your gown and wig? What do you think you're doing, lounging there like a lord! Do you want us to be taken up for travelling on a Sunday?'

The boy got to his feet, trying to look as though he wasn't hurrying.

'I shall have to go,' he said. 'They can do nothing without me.'

'Bestir yourself!' shouted the man, 'or I'll stir you with a thump of my fist! What? Are you to sit swilling ale, while we trudge to and fro like beasts of burden?'

The boy jumped down from the stage. '"Like will to like," said the devil to the collier,' he quoted impudently, and then dodged to avoid a cuff on the side of the head, and ran indoors.

'There goes your leading actor,' said William, looking after him.

Rufus was silent for a moment.

'Better than being apprenticed to a hatter,' he said.

'What?' said William in astonishment.

Rufus didn't look at him.

'I'm going away from Stratford,' he said. 'My uncle has apprenticed me to a hat-maker in Nottingham.'

'Oh, no!' William exclaimed.

'Oh, yes!' said Rufus mockingly. 'The indentures are signed and I'm travelling to Nottingham tomorrow with John Audley, my Master.'

The players were beginning to take down the stage now, and the boys moved away from the banging and hammering.

'You're leaving school then,' said William.

Rufus shrugged. 'Have left. Today was the last day. You know old Beetle-brows kept me behind? You'll never believe it, but he said that he was sorry I was going, and that he thought I was worthy of better things than hats.'

'And are you?'

William said it quite seriously, for he thought that no one really knew the answer except Rufus.

'I don't know,' replied Rufus, in the same way. He grinned. 'Now we shall never know. When you see me next, I shall be the complete hatter.' He put his hands together, and bowed in the doorway of an imaginary shop. 'Yes, sir. A hat like a pudding-basin? Certainly, sir. That should suit you perfectly, for you have a face like a pudding. What can I do for you, mistress? A hat exactly like your husband's, only twice as large, and with a feather in it? Here it is. Go away and snuff yourself with it, and when you're tired of it, you can use it for the candles.'

William laughed, but he thought that to Rufus it was not entirely a joke.

'What would you like to have done?' he asked.

'I don't know,' said Rufus again. 'But the world's a great place. There are our English discoverers, like Francis Drake and John Hawkins and Martin Frobisher, sailing all about the globe, from the Indies to Muscovy, bringing back strange tales, and great riches, so that everyone envies them, and wonders at it, and longs to go too. And here am I to be shut up in a hatter's shop for the rest of my life, like a bird in a felt cage.' He leant against the wall and watched the players, who in half an hour had built and now destroyed their imaginary kingdom. 'What would I like to do? I'd like to take ship and sail out into oceans no man has ever seen before, and never to come back, or else to come back rich beyond belief.' He looked at William, and laughed, and returned to the world they both knew. 'And if I'm going to be bound apprentice for seven years, I'd rather go to London than to Nottingham !'

'Richard Field is to be apprenticed to a printer in London,' said William.

'Yes, I know,' said Rufus.

'Master Hunt came to see my father,' said William. 'He thinks I might gain a scholarship and go to the University at Oxford. That's why he's been teaching me Greek. He says I should meet all sorts of great men at the University, and one of them might find me a place at Court.'

They were both silent for a moment. What could be said when William's future looked so bright, and Rufus' prospects were so dull?

'Well,' said Rufus, cheerfully, 'perhaps I shall win fame yet, by selling you hats.'

They walked out of the yard, past the large cart which the players were hitching up to two stout horses. Soon the company would set out from the inn, taking with them their stage and costumes and musical instruments, and follow the dusty roads to their next town. And after that would come the next town, and the next, until the autumn found them back in London, playing in inns or at the Theater in Shoreditch.

'I must hurry home to supper,' said Rufus, when he and William had passed under the archway into the street. 'My aunt is reversing the Bible story. She's killing the fatted calf for the Prodigal *before* he goes off to eat husks for seven years.'

'Joanne will miss you,' said William.

Rufus smiled.

'Tell her to talk all the time I'm gone,' he said, 'so that she'll be ready to be quiet and listen when I get back. Oh yes, and tell her that if I don't meet anyone better in Nottingham, I'll come back and marry her.'

'I thought you were going to marry a rich wife,' said William.

'That's right, I'd forgotten,' Rufus agreed. 'Tell her to learn lace-making, and earn some money, and save it till I come!'

And he went laughing down the road, just as so often before, when school was over and they were parting from each other until next morning. Only this time, William thought, they were parting for much longer. An apprentice was bound to his Master for seven years, to work for him, and learn the trade, living in the house and doing as he was told. Nottingham was a long way away, and William knew that many days would pass before Rufus came again to Stratford.

As William turned and walked past the inn door on his way home, he was stopped by someone breathlessly calling his name from inside. He turned back, and a little man with spectacles which slid down his nose, ran out, still holding a mug of ale in his hand.

'William!' he called. 'Young William Shakespeare, isn't it?'

'Master Wedgewood!' said William, pleased to recognize his old friend, the tailor.

'Did you see the play?' cried Master Wedgewood. 'What a sight! What a sight it was! Such clothes! And such rich jewels! That velvet gown, now, the purple one, fringed with gold, it cost more than a hundred pounds, I'll be sworn! And did you see the cloth of silver which the King wore?' He paused and shook his head, overcome by the memory of so much magnificence.

'I never knew a play was like that! If I'd known, I would have left my work, and come to see them all. Kings and queens on the stage – and princes, too – and some of them here in the inn, drinking ale, as friendly as you please! It's very wonderful.'

William hesitated.

'Er – they aren't really kings and queens, Master Wedgewood,' he said. 'They're – you know, they're actors, really, taking the part of kings and queens.'

Master Wedgewood considered the matter solemnly.

'Actors!' he said. 'Fancy that! And wearing those clothes and jewels and making those great speeches!' He poked his spectacles up with the tip of his forefinger, and peered into his ale, so that they slid down again, and then looked up at William over the top of them. 'It must be a great thing to be an actor,' he said.

'Yes,' said William, 'it must.'

But as he walked homewards, William thought of the Queen's Interluders, fallen on hard days, despised and forced to travel. He thought of the times when plague closed the theatres, or when the City Fathers would not let them play in London, or when audiences did not come, and there was no money, and how, unless they had a patron to protect them with his name as they travelled round the country, actors could be arrested as rogues and vagabonds and whipped or thrown into prison. And he thought of Rufus, ready with his apple-core if the play didn't please him. Altogether, in spite of the glories of an actor's life, the fine clothes, and the applause, William was glad that for him it was to be the University, and afterwards (for he knew that this was what he wanted most of all) the chance to live at Court, and to become a famous poet.

8

Sorrow

School was never quite the same again to William without
Rufus, and soon after this, Master Simon Hunt, too, left
Stratford. William had long since forgotten that he had
ever been afraid of him, and was very sad to see him go.
Some time later, they heard that Master Hunt had gone to
Douai, in France, and had become a Jesuit Priest. Many
people in Stratford spoke of him angrily, saying that he
was a traitor, and that the Roman Catholics were plotting
to murder Queen Elizabeth and put King Philip of Spain
on the throne. But William, remembering the fierce-
browed, tender-hearted schoolmaster, found that he could
not hate the Roman Catholics if Master Hunt was one of
them.

The new schoolmaster was quite different. His name
was Thomas Jenkins, and he was a Welshman, small,
dark and lively, speaking in a sing-song way, and always
saying things like 'pless' when he meant, 'bless', and
'effer', for 'ever'. But the boys all liked him, and although
he often said 'we must have discipline, boys, discipline!'
and threatened terrible beatings, he could hardly ever
bring himself to punish anyone, and usually ended by
making an impassioned speech about 'The peauties of the
Latin tongue,' and letting them all go home half an hour
early.

At Christmastime, the boys acted a Latin comedy by
Plautus. Master Jenkins spent happy hours rehearsing
them in it during school, crying out every few minutes,
'No, no, that iss not the way to do it! You have the accent
all wrong, boy! Use better discretion when you wave your
hand. You look as though you are herding sheep or cattle!
God pless the boy! I'll show you how to do it myself!'
However, all went well in the end. All the boys' parents
came to see the play as well as several gentlemen, like Sir
Thomas Lucy and Sir Fulke Greville, who lived nearby
and took an interest in the school. William played the
chief part, and won great praise for it. Even his mother,
as they walked home afterwards, said, 'You did very well,
William'; though she added, of course, 'Don't let it make
you proud!'

But somehow that Christmas was not a very cheerful
one at Henley Street. William thought perhaps it was
because little Nan was not well. She was growing very
thin, and had a troublesome cough which would not go,
for all Mary Shakespeare's dosing with liquorice and hore-
hound. But he could not help noticing, too, that his father
always seemed to come in from the shop in the evenings
with a worried look, and that the men who visited him
there were different now. Once they had been prosperous-
looking farmers, arranging sales of sheep and cattle to his
father, who used the skins for his business, and sold the
meat and wool. Now, William noticed more and more as
time went by that his father's visitors seemed to be quiet,
shabby men, with whom his father had long, anxious
talks, and who left at the end with unfriendly looks and
without any of those loud, cheery greetings which the
farmers used to send 'to the Mistress and the little ones.'
And perhaps even stranger still, his father, who in the
past had been Alderman, Bailiff and Chief Alderman of

the Town, had not attended council meetings now for more than two years.

But everything else was forgotten when Nan suddenly became very ill. She had always been such a delicate little thing that they had somehow become used to it, and thought that she was stronger than she looked, like a snowdrop which, for all its drooping, still lives through the cold February snows. But now it was different.

They were in the sitting-room, one evening in early April. It was fine and sunny, but still cold, so there was a wood fire burning. After the spring-cleaning, all the furniture had a special shine on it, and there were new rushes on the scrubbed wooden floor. Over the fireplace, the piece of tapestry, showing the visit of the Queen of Sheba to King Solomon, was as bright as when John Shakespeare first bought it in Warwick, the year he was Chief Alderman.

The apothecary had been to the house earlier in the day, and the Minister, too, had come to pray that Nan might get better. Now Joanne and her mother were upstairs with Nan, and William and Gilbert sat reading, while their father mended Richard's toy cart. Richard himself, five years old, rosy, happy and destructive, set his wooden soldiers up in rows, and then, with imaginary cannon-shots, knocked them clattering down.

Suddenly, from upstairs, they heard Mary Shakespeare's voice calling, 'John! Husband! Come quickly!' Their father flung down the cart, and ran up the stairs. William and Gilbert put down their books and stood up, looking at each other. For a while, there was no sound from up-stairs, and then they heard Joanne burst out crying, and a few minutes later their father came, slowly and heavily, downstairs, and stood there without speaking, and they knew that their little sister was dead.

William went by himself up Welcombe Hill. He thought how strange it was that while all the rest of them would grow up and go out into the world, and become, in a way, different people, Nan would never change. They would always think of her as the same gentle little girl, sitting beside Joanne with her sewing, or nursing the painted wooden doll she called her 'baby', or joining in the family music in the evenings with her thin, light voice. Even years afterwards, when he was, perhaps, a famous poet, and Gilbert a lawyer in London, and Joanne married with children of her own, still that was how they would think of her, their own beloved little Nan. And somehow this was a comfort to him.

9

Troubles

One Sunday, a few weeks after William's fifteenth birthday, they were all getting dressed to go to Church, when Gilbert, who, as usual, was ready first and standing by the window, said, 'I wonder who those men are, out there.'

'What men?' asked his father, sharply. His mother was just helping Richard into his doublet (or rather, Gilbert's handed down!). She stayed quite still where she was, stooped over him, while Richard looked up into her face in surprise.

'Two men,' said Gilbert. 'They're standing in the doorway of the shop, as though they were sheltering from the rain. Only it's not raining,' he added.

William turned towards the window, but his father stopped him.

'Wait!' he said. 'Don't – don't let them see you!'

William stayed where he was, astonished to see his father move in a furtive way along the wall, until he could look out of the window, over Gilbert's shoulder.

'There's someone else in the doorway opposite,' said Gilbert, still casually glancing out, as though he merely had nothing better to do.

His father turned away. He took off the tall hat, his best one, in which he always went to Church, and laid it down on the chest in silence. Mary Shakespeare straightened, looking at him.

'What is it?' she asked. 'Who are they?'

He didn't answer her, but only said, 'I can't go out. You must go without me.'

'But you must go to Church!' cried Mary Shakespeare. 'It's—it's Sunday! And you don't want to be presented before the Courts for not attending service! Don't let's add that to our other troubles!'

'It's better than being arrested and put in prison,' said John Shakespeare.

William looked at his father in horror.

'Father, what do you mean?' he cried.

'Be quiet!' said his father, in a tone he had never heard from him before. 'Do as I say, all of you. Go to Church without me. Say nothing to anyone on the way there.'

'Shall I fetch Audrey?' asked Joanne.

For Margery had married a shepherd, and gone to live at Charlecote, but Audrey was still with them.

Mary Shakespeare finished dressing Richard, pulling his girdle tight with such a tug that he gasped.

'Yes,' she said. 'Fetch Audrey, and tell her to hold her tongue, for if she starts prattling I shall box her ears!'

By the time Joanne returned, with Audrey looking for once sensibly dressed in her plain gown, linen coif and woollen cap, the others were ready to leave. Warned by Joanne, Audrey certainly said nothing, but she exasperated her mistress by tip-toeing into the room as though they were all conspirators, and were planning a robbery. If she had been wearing a cloak, Mary Shakespeare felt sure she would have pulled the hood over her face, and made secret signs under it with her fingers.

Gilbert had stayed where he was, by the window.

'Where are they now?' asked his father.

'One of them is looking at his watch. Now they're moving closer.'

'Very well,' said his father. 'Richard, take your mother's hand. William, take your mother's arm on the other side, and be ready to open the door when I say. Joanne, you go next with Audrey, and keep close to the others. Gilbert, you go last, and shut the door behind you. Whatever you do, don't let them get inside the doorway.'

They all got ready to do as he said. In spite of his bewilderment and anxiety, William could not help finding it all rather exciting, and he knew by Joanne's face that she did, too.

'Are you ready?' said their father. 'Now remember what I say. Don't speak to anyone, and don't stop on the way. Very well, William.'

William opened the door and stepped outside with his mother and Richard, and found the two men on the doorstep, so that they had to jostle their way past them, with Joanne and Audrey close behind. Before they were fairly out of the door, one of the men, a big, burly fellow, shouted, 'John Shakespeare, I arrest you at the suit of—' and then stopped short, as he saw Gilbert closing the door behind them. He and the other man stood threateningly in front of them.

'Where is he?' said one of them. 'We're officers of the law, and we have a warrant. Where is he?'

'Stand aside!' cried William, angrily, and let go of his mother's arm to draw his dagger.

'Weapons, is it?' said the other man, and put his hand to his sword.

But Mary Shakespeare, taking a firmer grip of Richard's hand, stepped forward with such determination that the men gave way, and William, remembering what his father had said, let his dagger slip back into its sheath and took her arm again. They began to march away down the road, like a solid little Shakespeare army, but at that the third man, who had been lurking in a doorway opposite, came running across the road, calling out, 'Stop them! Don't let them go! Officers, do your duty! Arrest him!'

'How can we arrest him when he isn't here?' demanded one of the officers, irritably.

'Fetch him out!' cried the man, who was thin-faced and sharp-nosed and looked like a weasel. 'He's there in the house. Fetch the villain out!'

William and Gilbert looked at each other, and at their mother, and, with one accord, they all stopped short.

'You know we're not allowed to break into the house,' said the other officer. 'We can only take him up on the streets. But he'll have to come out sooner or later, and the moment he sets foot out of doors, we'll have him, never fear!'

There were several people about by now, setting out for Church, and they stared curiously at the little group.

'Let us go on,' said Mary Shakespeare, in a low, hurried voice.

But as they set off again, the thin-faced man took a few steps after them, calling, 'He owes me forty pounds! I'm a poor man! Why should he rob me of such a sum as that? He is a thief!'

They were all walking on, as though they hadn't heard, but at this, to their horror, Audrey stopped and shrieked back in her shrill voice, 'Shame on your heart to say so! He's as honest a man as you and I, in fact he's more honest than you are, for you say he's not honest, and that's a lie, I'll be sworn!'

'Don't, Audrey, don't!' cried Joanne, trying to tug her along.

'He's a villain!' shouted the man, and then, at the top of his lungs, 'John Shakespeare is a villain!'

'He's not!' cried Richard. He suddenly broke free from his mother and rushed towards the man, drawing the little dagger which, being the youngest, and spoiled, he had been given much sooner than the others. 'My father isn't a villain!' he roared, red in the face, and with tears in his eyes.

'Richard! No! Stop him!' cried his mother, and Gilbert, moving very quickly for one who was usually so leisurely, caught hold of Richard, and swiftly took the dagger from him and swung him round, and they all walked on again in silence. There was no fun or excitement left in any of it now. It was terrible to see the curious stares of their neighbours, and one or two smiles, as the man still stood in the middle of the road, shouting after them that he would have justice, and that he had waited long enough for his money, and would be fobbed off no further.

They none of them spoke, all the way down Henley Street, but as they turned the corner, Mary Shakespeare said, 'When your father was prosperous, that fellow was glad enough to lend him money, and begged and begged to be allowed to do so, and to share in the profits of the business. But now that there are losses, he won't share those.'

*

When they came out of Church after the service, Adrian Quiney came bustling up, calling out, 'God be with you, Mistress Shakespeare! Where is your husband? Not at Church? Is he ill?'

William saw his mother draw herself together for a moment, as though she was about to make a great effort, and then she replied, quietly but firmly, 'Yes. He is not well this morning.' William knew that it was the first lie she had ever told.

It was a useless lie, too, he knew, because Audrey, sitting in the gallery of the Church with the other servants, would by now have whispered the whole story to them. In Stratford, where servants lived and ate and slept with the family, it would in a few hours be known all over the town.

'We will walk with you part of the way,' said Adrian Quiney, in his fussy way. 'What is wrong with him? A spring chill, I suppose. He should take care. Now, let's see. He is of the sanguine humour. He should avoid leeks. Tell him not to eat any leeks until he is recovered. I dare swear that is what has done the damage. Now I am of the phlegmatic humour. Leeks do not harm me at all.'

'I think a drink of aniseed is very good for the rheum,' said Mistress Quiney in her plaintive voice.

If every man and woman could really be classed in different kinds of temperament, and dosed accordingly, she was certainly among those of the melancholy humour, and, by Master Quiney's rules should never have touched hare, goat-meat, pigeons, peas or beans, though in fact she ate them all, and afterwards complained no more than usual.

'No, no,' said Master Quiney, 'aniseed is only the cure. It is the cause, it is the cause that one must find. Depend upon it, the cause is leeks, nothing but leeks.'

The Quineys were so happily engaged, all the way home, in prescribing for John Shakespeare's illness that they never noticed how quiet the rest of the family was, and parted from them comfortably certain that they had given a great deal of valuable advice.

In Henley Street, there was no sign of the man who was claiming his money, though the two officers who were there to serve his writ were leaning against a wall opposite the house. Mary Shakespeare walked more quickly, and William thought at first that they were going to get inside without any more trouble, but as he opened the door, the big, burly officer straightened up and shouted across the road,

'Tell him to come out! He must come out sometime! We can wait. We'll get him in the end! Tell him to come out!'

Other people strolling home from Church, stopped and stared.

'Get inside quickly!' said Mary Shakespeare.

She bundled Richard in before her, and the others followed, with William coming last to shut the door. John Shakespeare was sitting by the fire. He didn't move, or turn his head, as they came in, and for a moment they all stood and looked at each other, with a dreadfully trapped feeling, like a besieged garrison. Then Mary Shakespeare straightened her shoulders, took off her hat and gave it to Joanne to carry upstairs, and took down her apron from behind the door.

'Well, Audrey,' she said, 'you had better come and baste the meat, if we are to have any dinner today. There's no need to meet trouble half-way. We'll eat while we can.'

She set off for the kitchen, followed by Audrey, and William sighed in relief, and caught Gilbert's eye, and smiled.

'If Hell were to open before Mother's feet,' he said, 'her first thought would be that hell-fire was just right for roasting beef.'

'Yes,' Gilbert agreed. 'And she'd set the Devil to turning the spit with his pitchfork!'

But though they all tried to make it seem like an ordinary day, they could none of them forget how it had begun. It was a relief when it rained in the afternoon, and the two officers, tired of the cascades of water which poured down their necks from the gutters, went quietly away.

'They'll be back soon,' said John Shakespeare, and he didn't venture out with the rest of the family to evening service.

After supper, when Richard, Joanne and Audrey were in bed, William and Gilbert knew that the time had come for them to learn what it all meant. It was a dull, rainy evening, but although Audrey had brought in the candles, they were not yet lit. John Shakespeare still sat in his chair by the fire, and Mary Shakespeare, on the chest by the window, caught the last of the light for her mending. William and Gilbert sat on their stools and waited. It seemed as though their father was never going to begin, but at last he raised his head to look at them, and said, 'Well, boys, you see how it is. I have no money, and what is worse, I am in debt.'

Gilbert nodded, as though satisfied, but William could not help saying, 'But, Father, how did it happen?'

'I don't know,' said his father. 'I don't know. I lent money to farmers, so that they could buy more land and better beasts, and so that I could make a better profit for all of us. And when that succeeded, then I lent more money, and supplied wool to cottage weavers, so that they could make the cloth and pay me later, and as I undertook more commissions, then other men, seeing me prosperous, lent money for me to lay out for them. And then there was disease among the cattle and sheep, and a mortgage was foreclosed, so that one of my men lost his land and couldn't repay me, and some of the weavers couldn't sell their cloth, and so I couldn't repay the money I had borrowed, and trade fell away through foreign glove-makers, and now – now it's all gone. I'm like a man who has sent all his fortune out on the sea in merchant ships, and has seen them all founder one by one. Everything has gone now!'

Mary Shakespeare rolled up the pair of linen stockings she was mending, and folded her hands in her lap.

'Not everything,' she said. 'We have the two houses to sell, and the land at Wilmcote and Snitterfield.'

William looked at his mother quickly. The land at Wilmcote and Snitterfield was her own inheritance from her father, and with it went the Arden family house, Asbies, where she was born.

'No!' cried John Shakespeare. 'I'm not selling those lands! They're to go to William. What would he be if we sold those? Nothing but a tradesman, like his father. How can I get the grant of a coat of arms unless we have some land in the family? I want my son to write "gentleman" after his name.'

'Someone else will write "dead of starvation" after it," said Mary Shakespeare, briskly, 'unless your debts are paid, and there is some money coming into the house.'

William smiled a little at that, but his father said obstinately, 'I won't sell those lands.'

'We must mortgage, then,' said his wife. 'My brother, Edmund Lambert, will lend us money upon them, I'm sure of that.'

John Shakespeare sighed.

'Very well,' he said, 'we'll mortgage the lands.'

He was silent again, staring into the fire, and William thought that his mother looked at him with some impatience. Then she put her mending away and came to sit on the oak settle, saying, 'It is getting quite dark. Gilbert, light the candles.'

Gilbert did so, with a rush taper which he lit at the fire, and as the tallow flared (for Mary Shakespeare made her own candles, of course, from fat, rendered down, and only used wax candles for special occasions) she said, 'Now, about the boys—'

William's moment of amusement was past. He felt his heart beating, and knew what was coming, and yet he still felt a sickening shock of disappointment when his father, rousing himself, said, 'It means leaving school at once.'

'But—the University!' cried William.

His father glanced at his mother, as though to get some courage, before he said gently, 'You see, William, it is impossible. Even though you were given a scholarship, there are the books and clothes, and other expenses, and besides, I need your help in the business.'

The two apprentices had before this completed their indentures, and were employed in the shop by the day, as journeymen.

'I must let the men go,' said his father, 'and you must take their place.'

William felt as though a trap was slowly closing upon him. He wanted to cry out, and leap to his feet and rush out of the house. He remembered what Rufus had said about the hatter's shop closing upon him for the rest of his life, like a felt cage. And now here he was himself in the same position, only his was to be the leather cage of a glover's shop.

'Oh, Father!' he cried, despairingly.

He saw his father turn his head away quickly, but his mind was in such a turmoil of protest that he could not think of any pain but his own. He said, in a wild attempt to escape the trap, 'When the lands are mortgaged, Father, wouldn't it be possible?'

'The mortgage would only pay my immediate debts,' said John Shakespeare. 'I'm sorry for it, William.'

He spoke very wearily, and William, struggling against his bitter disappointment, managed to say, 'It doesn't matter, Father.' And then, more heartily, for, indeed, he felt it *did* matter, but this at least was true, 'It can't be helped.'

His mother turned and smiled at him, with tears in her eyes, and he felt more than repaid. Then he suddenly remembered something.

'But Gilbert!' he cried. 'What about Gilbert?'

'Gilbert must leave school as well,' said his father. His voice was more cheerful now. 'We must all work very hard, and no doubt we shall soon begin to prosper again.'

'But—he was going to London, to study law at Clement's Inn,' cried William.

'No, that is not to be thought of,' said his father. 'There is no money for it, and anyway I shall need him here.'

All this time, Gilbert had said nothing. William turned and looked at him. It was bad enough for himself, but how much worse it must be for Gilbert, who was a much more brilliant scholar, who had been able to read and write before he was five, and knew his Latin grammar before he was eight, and who had known so early that what he wanted to do was to go to London and enter one of the Inns of Chancery, and become a lawyer. The light flared to and fro on his dark, thin face, almost as though there was a fire inside it, which raged, and then died down. Then he said at last, 'If it must be so, it must.' And that was the last word he ever spoke about the ending of all his ambitions.

10

The Gentleman in the Shop

'There's the officer again,' said Joanne, looking out of the window.

'Which one?' asked William.

'Master Fang.'

This was the big man. They called him that because he looked like a mastiff, one of those rather stupid fighting dogs who never let go once they have taken hold. They had nicknamed the other one Snare, because he was little and mean-looking, and they felt sure that he could never catch anyone in fair fight but only by setting traps.

'It's just as well Father went out by the back way,' Joanne remarked.

'Unless Snare is waiting there,' said William.

'Oh well, Father has a horse, and he hasn't,' said Joanne hopefully.

For Master Hornby sometimes hired out horses, as well as shoeing them, and had left one ready for John Shakespeare tied to a fence near the Guild Pits.

William, who was working at his father's accounts, laid down his pen.

'If you're in debt,' he said, 'you always want to pay what you owe to the butcher and the blacksmith, so that you can eat, and run. Father sells meat himself, so he only has to pay the blacksmith.'

Joanne smiled. She and William were alone in the shop. Gilbert had gone to the market, and their father was riding out of town on business – if he could slip past the officers.

'It's a whole year since the officers first came,' said Joanne. 'Do you remember how frightened we were?'

'Yes,' said William. 'But *then* we thought that they would soon be gone.'

'Well, they did go—' said Joanne.

'Yes,' said William, 'but they came back.'

They both sighed, and looked at each other, and laughed, and then stopped laughing.

'I don't think Uncle Lambert lent Father enough money on the Wilmcote land,' said Joanne.

'No,' William agreed, 'I don't think he did. But it wouldn't have made much difference. With all the other debts, and with Uncle Henry Shakespeare getting into difficulties, and having to be helped out of them, and with the wool trade in a bad way—'

'— and with the price of everything going up all the time—' Joanne put in, mimicking her mother, and they both laughed again.

They thought of the wonderful few weeks after Uncle Lambert lent the forty pounds. It was to be paid back in a year's time, or else the land would become their uncle's, and at first their father had talked about repaying the money within a few months. But if he had managed to save, it was only by leaving other debts unpaid. It was a black day when they looked out of the window, and saw Master Fang and Master Snare once more lurking in the doorway, and when William had named them that, they had all been glad to laugh, not because it was really so funny, but because they wanted to pretend that it wasn't shameful to owe money which you couldn't pay, and that they weren't really afraid of the officers at all. But it was, and they were.

'It's like being in prison,' said Joanne turning back to the window. 'Fang and Snare are the gaolers, walking up and down outside, and father's debts are the bolts on the door. Your dungeon is the workshop, and mine is the kitchen. Do you think we shall ever escape?'

'You will,' said William. 'You'll be getting married in a few years' time.'

'Shall I?' asked Joanne. 'I don't know. Father won't have any money now for a marriage settlement.'

'Well—' said William.

It was perfectly true, of course, that a father who was arranging his son's marriage would always prefer to marry him to a girl who had some money or land as a dowry.

'Perhaps some rich young man will fall in love with you,' he said.

'I doubt it,' answered Joanne, gloomily. 'I'm not beautiful.'

'Well—' said William again.

To be fashionable, a girl had to have red hair, like the Queen, but to be beautiful she must have golden hair and grey eyes. Joanne's hair was dark and curly, and her eyes, like his and like their mother's, were hazel.

'I know what I shall do,' said Joanne, putting her chin on her fist and glaring out of the window in a determined way. 'I shall do the same as the girl in that story you read. I shall take a bottle of mother's medicine, and I shall go up to London, and the Queen will be very ill, and I shall cure her.'

'Mother's spring medicine would cure anyone of anything,' said William.

'And then,' Joanne went on with growing enthusiasm,

D

'the Queen will say to me, "You see all the rich gentle-men at my Court. You can choose whichever one you like for your husband."'

'And which one will you choose?' enquired William.

'Oh, any one,' answered Joanne, carelessly. 'I don't mind. And he will build me a great big house just out-side Stratford, with tapestries hanging on the walls in every room – and – and – and silver and gold dishes *every-where,* and we will all go and live there.'

'What, all of us?' exclaimed William, much amused. 'What will your husband say?'

'Oh, he will die,' said Joanne, 'as soon as we're married. I only want him for the house and money. And we shall all live there for the rest of our lives, as merry as can be, and when Uncle Lambert asks me to lend him some money, I shall say, "Yes, but you must be more careful in future!"'

William chuckled. That was what their uncle had said to their father, as he plonked the leather bag of money on the table in front of him, and it had annoyed them all very much.

'That's what I shall do,' said Joanne, with satisfaction. 'What will you do, Will?'

'I don't know,' William answered.

He suddenly couldn't make a joke of it any longer, and he was glad when their mother called Joanne to come and help her in the kitchen, where she was making brawn for the winter, from the tame boar which she had raised in the back yard. Joanne's task was always to prepare the spices.

'Ugh! Back to my dungeon!' said Joanne. 'And I don't even like brawn!'

She went cheerfully off to the kitchen. Joanne could never stay gloomy or cross for long, and always laughed herself into a good humour again in a few minutes. When she was gone, William got up from the desk, and walked impatiently up and down the room. It was different for Joanne. There wasn't anything a girl could do except work in the house. Even if their father were very rich, it would only mean that she would do fine needlework instead of hemming sheets, and walk in the rose-garden instead of making brawn. But for him the loss of his father's money was like a heavy iron door shutting in his face. He thought of all his plans for going to the University, and meeting scholars, and nobles, and great men from overseas. He remembered how he had hoped to go to Court and be given some place in the Queen's household, and that he had planned to become her own poet, envied and admired by the whole country. And here he was, in the dark shop in Henley Street, writing down figures about the price of wool and the cost of leather. Joanne had called it a prison. He felt like a prince who had once been heir to a rich and glorious kingdom, and now was shut up in a narrow dungeon, to live out his life without hope or pleasure, as best he might.

It was warm and stuffy in the shop. William went to the door and pushed it open, and saw Fang start and look round hopefully, and then turn away again. In the street, a gentleman was walking idly up and down, evidently waiting for his horse to be shod, but William hardly noticed him. He couldn't bear to go back to working on his accounts, and he took up his father's lute which always lay on a stool in the corner. In the happy old days, his father's customers would often pick it up in turn and play and sing, and they used to say that the glover's shop in Henley Street was more tuneful than the barber's, where a lute always hung ready for those who were waiting to be shaved. But now his father hardly ever played the lute, and only William and Gilbert would occasionally take it in turns to sing to it in the evening, while the other played the recorder.

William sat down on a stool by the door, where a slight breeze came in, and began to play and sing to himself quietly, trying to forget everything except the song and the music. In a little while, he had lost himself in it so completely that he was very much startled when a voice nearby said, 'Whose song is that?'

He looked up and saw a gentleman standing in the doorway, and answered quickly, 'Mine, sir!'

'Bless the boy!' cried the gentleman, laughing, 'I didn't think you had stolen it! You bought it from some pedlar, I daresay, in the market. Have you the sheet of music there?'

William stood up, suddenly remembering his manners, and answered, 'No, sir. It's – I made it up.'

'The words, or the tune?' enquired the gentleman, idly enough, preparing to walk on again.

'Both, sir,' William answered.

It was, in fact, a poem which he had written when Nan died, and he himself had set a tune to it. The gentleman paused.

'Indeed?' he said. He turned back. 'You have a pleasing voice, and a good accent,' he said. 'What is your name? It's so dark in there that I can't see you, after the brightness of the sunlight.'

'William Shakespeare, sir.'

The gentleman stepped inside the shop.

'The glover's son?' he said. He was a pleasant-looking man of middle-age, with a beard and moustache going grey, and William saw at once that his clothes, though not fantastical or extravagant, were of rich material and fashionably cut. He looked at William more closely.

'Haven't I seen you before?' he enquired. 'I think I know you.'

'I don't think—' William began, but the gentleman exclaimed, laughing, 'Of course! It was in the comedy of Plautus which was acted at the school. You played the chief part, I think.'

'Yes, sir,' William answered and remembered that this was the gentleman who had been pointed out to him then as Sir Fulke Greville.

'Your Master talked to me about you,' said Sir Fulke. 'He seemed to have great hopes for you. So your father has put you to his own trade, has he?'

William thought how little had come of his Masters' 'hopes' for him, and he hung his head and didn't answer. When the gentleman spoke again, his voice was stern.

'Come, boy, there is no need to be ashamed of being a tradesman! If you have learnt *that* at school, you have been badly taught! And perhaps, instead of praising you for singing well, I should have scolded you for being idle in your father's shop. It is the duty of a child to obey its parents. If your father wishes you to become a craftsman like himself, then you should work hard and be a credit to him.'

'But—he—he doesn't wish it, sir,' said William.

'Hey? Well, then, why are you here?'

William glanced uneasily up at the gentleman, but could find no words to answer. At that moment Snare came through the passage from Guild Street.

'Well, did you see him?' shouted Fang, in his usual baying roar.

'No,' piped Snare. 'They say he's ridden out of town!'

'A murrain on him!' shouted Fang. 'Well, we'll get him when he returns, never fear!'

Part of the revenge they took for being made to wait about all day in the street was to carry on all their con-

versation at the top of their voices, so that everyone should
know that they were there to arrest John Shakespeare for
debt. Sir Fulke went to the door and looked at Fang and
Snare, and then he turned and spoke to William with a
new kindness.

'Ah yes, I see,' he said. 'I had heard that your father
was in difficulties. Sir Thomas Lucy told me of them.
I am very sorry. I know they are caused by misfortune
and not by folly or misbehaviour. And this, no doubt, has
made some difference to his plans for you.'

' "Some difference" !' thought William, but he answered
only, 'Yes, sir.'

'H'm !' said Sir Fulke.

He came back inside the shop, and took a stool and sat
down. Holding his sword between his knees, and looking
up at William thoughtfully, he began to ask him questions, such as how old he was, and what he had learnt at
school, and how he spent his spare time.

'Those are good answers,' he said at last, standing up.
'I need not ask you if you are honest and sober and truthful, for with that father, you could not be otherwise.'

William felt a glow of pride to know that, even with
Fang and Snare at the door, his father's good name still
counted for so much, but he wondered why a gentleman
who scarcely knew him, and who did not even live in
Stratford, should take such an interest in him, and he was
even more puzzled when Sir Fulke went on,

'Your father is out of town this morning. Will he have
returned by this afternoon?'

'Yes, sir,' William answered, and silently added to himself, 'if he can get past Snare at the back door.'

'Very well,' said Sir Fulke. 'I am dining in Stratford
with a friend. Tell your father that I should like to see him
after dinner, and that I will visit him here.'

'Yes, sir,' said William.

He was still standing in the same place by the door, holding the lute, as the gentleman stepped out into the street. He saw Sir Fulke walk up to Fang and Snare and speak to them, and then, without another glance in William's direction, walk past the shop again towards the smithy.

*

When William's father returned, Fang and Snare were nowhere to be seen, and William wondered if it was because the gentleman had spoken to them. His father was as puzzled as he was to know why Sir Fulke Greville should want to see him, for he had only met him once or twice about some council business, and that was all finished long since.

William's mother said the only thing that mattered to her was that he *was* coming, and might come into the sitting-room. She hustled them all through dinner and had the table moved almost as the last mouthfuls were swallowed. Then she set to work with Audrey, cleaning and polishing, sweeping the floor, and putting fresh rushes down (though the new ones weren't due for another week), and mixing them with lavender and rosemary, which she did only on holidays and for important guests. The tapestry had been sold some time since, and most of her best silver and pewter, but a painted cloth now hung over the fireplace, and as she surveyed the bare, sweet-smelling room, she said, 'There! Now the Queen herself may come, if she likes.'

'*Will* the Queen come, Mother?' asked Richard, who always took everything very literally.

'I don't know,' answered his mother calmly, 'but she called and had supper with Mistress Thomas Fisher, who lives near Kenilworth, some seven years ago, and never gave her a word of warning, so she might do the same with us one day. Meanwhile, if Sir Fulke Greville comes in here, I am ready for him too!'

In fact, Sir Fulke went first into the shop. They heard him arrive, and William ran out to hold his stirrup. The groom, who rode with him, dismounted, too, and led the horses up and down the street, while Sir Fulke and John Shakespeare went inside.

'What can he want?' said William, going back into the house.

'Nothing important to us, I daresay,' answered his mother, satisfied to know that the brawn was soaking in its sauce of beer and spices and could look after itself. 'Joanne, here is this holland which I bought cheap in the market. I cut it out last night, and if you take small turnings, it will make you two smocks. You can start them now and I will help you.'

Gilbert, delighted to be momentarily released from the shop, had sat down by the window with his book, stopping his reading now and then to help Richard with his letters. Gilbert had made up his mind that Richard should know how to read and write even if he never went to school, but it was a hard struggle teaching a child who after three months could not tell the difference between 'a' and 'b', and only Gilbert would have persevered with it.

William dawdled by the doorway, wondering again why Sir Fulke had asked him so many questions. It was very quiet in the room, with Joanne and his mother stitching, and Gilbert reading, and Richard pretending to learn his letters, but actually working loose the frame of the horn book with his thumb-nail. William said again, 'I wonder what he wants to see Father for.'

'William!' exclaimed his mother. 'It is no concern of

yours what he wants. Instead of fidgeting there, and being idle, you can spend the time usefully by going and weeding my herb garden.'

'Gilbert is just as idle,' said Joanne. 'He is only reading for his own pleasure.'

'I daresay,' said Mary Shakespeare, 'but he has the wit to do it quietly. Go on, William. Do as you're told!'

Gilbert read steadily on, with only a faint twitch at the corner of his mouth to show that he had heard, and William, feeling rather rebellious, went out into the garden. The sun was hot, and weeding the herb-garden was a job they all hated, because it meant stooping down so low. It seemed a long time later that Joanne came, solemn-faced, to call him. 'Has he gone?' William asked, and Joanne shook her head.

Inside, he found Sir Fulke sitting in his father's chair, while his mother and father stood together by the fire-place looking solemn also. Joanne went into the kitchen, and he saw that Gilbert and Richard had gone through into the shop. It was suddenly alarming to have their quiet family life interrupted in this way, and this hand-somely dressed gentleman taking possession of their living-room, like one of those messengers from the gods in Latin poems who come to order men, against their will, to perform hard tasks and undertake deeds of courage.

William took off his cap to Sir Fulke and bowed, but it was his father who spoke first.

'William,' he said, 'Sir Fulke has offered to take you into his household as his page.'

I I

Beauchamp Court

A few days later, William was riding out of Stratford on the Alcester Road, on his way to Beauchamp Court.

'You would live in my household,' Sir Fulke had said, 'and eat at my table. I should expect you to serve me in every way, to run errands for me, ride with me, hold my purse and write my letters. I should ask you to do no menial tasks, but you would have to rise early and go to bed late, to travel when I travel and to await my pleasure at home. I should expect absolute obedience, but I think you would find that I know how to reward faithful service. Are you willing to come?'

It did not seem to be a very attractive prospect, and yet William replied, without any hesitation, 'Yes, sir.' Now, as he rode along the dusty road, beside the servant who had come to fetch him, and who hadn't spoken a word since they left Stratford, he was wondering why he had agreed so readily.

'Is Sir Fulke a good master?' he asked.

'You'll find out!' replied the servant, and then, taking pity on William's look of dismay, he grinned and added, 'There's no better in England.'

'And Lady Anne?' enquired William.

He knew that Sir Fulke Greville's wife was the daughter of the Earl of Westmorland. He had so often heard the name of Westmorland in stories of famous battles handed down from his grandfather that he found it strange and exciting to think that he would soon be speaking to her, and living in the same house.

'Our mistress?' said the servant, whose name William discovered was Thomas, 'No one kinder while all goes well, but when it doesn't – hoo!'

William wondered what 'hoo!' meant, but he thought perhaps he had better not ask any more. They rode at a brisk pace and to William, enjoying the good horse and half reluctant to arrive, it seemed a very short time before they had passed Alcester and were turning in through the great gate and riding up an avenue of trees to the house. They crossed the bridge over the moat, and clattered into the cobbled stable yard, where they dismounted. The servant, unstrapping William's travelling bag from his own horse, said, 'You can go straight in. I'll see to your horse and bring your luggage.'

But William lingered, suddenly feeling that Thomas was his only friend in the world.

'Shall I ask for Sir Fulke?' he asked.

'No, the master's out riding. You'd better ask for Michael Malet.'

'Michael—?' enquired William.

Thomas suddenly made an extraordinary face, pulling down the corners of his mouth, opening his eyes very wide, and flaring out his nostrils, until he looked like an elderly owl, indignant at the smallness of the fieldmouse he had caught.

'Michael Malet,' he said. 'Steward. You'll see!'

And he dumped William's bag on the cobbles and began to unsaddle the horses.

William walked round the house, found the main door invitingly open, and went in. He was in the hall, a huge, oak-panelled room, which made the Stratford Council

Chamber look like a parlour. Right down the centre stood a heavy oak table and about a dozen servants, wearing a blue livery, were bustling up and down, setting places for dinner.

'They must be going to have a banquet,' thought William. 'Or else there are distinguished visitors coming.'

He began to feel more nervous than ever, and to wish that he had arrived on a day when they were having an ordinary family dinner. And then an even more alarming thought struck him. Perhaps this was the way the Grevilles always ate their dinner – with a damask table-cloth and so much silver plate, and a knife and fork at every place!

The butler came in from the door at the other end, beside the staircase, and all the servants suddenly began to move about twice as fast.

'Come, come, where are the rest of the trencher-plates?' he shouted. 'There should be one to every place. Peter, you idle fellow, didn't I tell you to fetch them from the cupboard? Take those glasses away and wash them! Someone has touched them with greasy fingers. What would my lady say if she saw them? Take the knife-case away. Gregory, help me to set out the salt.'

William stood and watched, fascinated, as an enormous silver saltcellar was lifted into the middle of the table. In his own family, they had a handsome pewter saltcellar, in the shape of an hour-glass, and were rather proud of it. But this one was four times as large, made of solid silver, and almost in the shape of a church, with a tall cover like a steeple, dotted with mother-of-pearl.

William was watching so intently while the butler and Gregory lifted this wonderful object on to the table, that he quite forgot that he was supposed to be asking for Master Malet, and he was taken by surprise, when a voice behind him said, 'Here, you! Fellow!'

He turned round, hardly believing that the voice could be addressing him. He had never in his life been called 'Fellow!' He saw a thin-faced, thin-lipped young man, dressed very soberly in black, whose nose came down towards his mouth, very much like an owl's. No doubt about it, William thought, remembering Thomas's imitation. This was Master Malet.

'What are you doing here?' demanded the steward. 'If you have brought a message, you should have gone to the kitchen. What do you want?'

William was so amazed that he forgot his nervousness, and answered, 'You are mistaken, sir. My name is William Shakespeare, and I am Sir Fulke's page.'

'Well, that's as may be—' began Master Malet.

'It is not "as may be",' William interrupted. 'It *is* so!'

'Umph!' said the steward, and obviously couldn't think of another way to start his sentence. Then he began again, 'Well—well, you should have asked for me first. I am steward of Sir Fulke's household.' He looked William up and down. 'Are you to wear a livery?'

'I don't know,' William answered. He thought to himself that there was only one livery he wanted to wear and that was the red one worn by the servants of the Queen. But he didn't say so.

'If you are to be with Sir Fulke, you must be dressed in a more seemly manner than *that*,' said Master Malet. 'That is most certain.'

William felt extremely angry. His family's wardrobe had been ransacked, so that he should be neatly dressed, and if Gilbert's doublet was rather small, and his father's embroidered shirt rather large, what right had Master Malet to sniff at them? But his mother's training helped him now to hold his tongue, however angry he was.

'Sir Fulke is not at home,' said Master Malet, 'but that

is no reason for you to be idle. You had better help the butler to set out the tables.'

William felt sure that this was not part of his duties, but he knew how powerful the steward of a great household could be, and he didn't want to quarrel with Master Malet any more than he had already. So he was just getting ready to do as he was told when there was an interruption.

Most of the servants had disappeared through the door which led to the kitchens, like bees vanishing into a bee-hive, and there was a momentary lull in the clatter they were making. In the silence a voice spoke from the top of the stairs.

'Michael! Is Sir Fulke's page there?'

It was a lady's voice, very sweet, and exceedingly firm.

Michael Malet hurried towards the staircase, calling out with anxious politeness, 'Yes, my lady! The boy is here, my lady!'

'Let him come up.'

Master Malet turned back to William in a busy fluster.

'It is my lady!' he whispered.

(William had guessed as much.)

'She wants you to go upstairs.'

(So much William had heard for himself.)

'Take off your cap and bow when you see her,' said Master Malet, hustling him towards the stairs. 'Don't speak until you are spoken to, and when you do, speak low. My lady hates loud voices. Oh, and do try to walk *quietly*!' he moaned. 'Those *shoes*!'

William, making, certainly, rather a clatter on the polished wood with his heavy leather shoes (only a year old, and newly soled) went up the stairs.

He didn't quite know what he expected to see. He knew, of course, that he would find himself in the gallery. It was a long room, with windows on one side looking out over the gardens. The ceiling was beautifully carved and gilded, and while some of the windows were plain and stood open to the light summer breeze, others were of stained glass. There were rich tapestries on the other wall, and scattered all about were stools and little tables, with lutes on them, and fine embroidery, books in velvet covers, a mother-of-pearl writing table and a jewelled comfit-box. But all this he saw later. When he first arrived at the top of the stairs he could see nothing but Lady Anne.

She sat in a carved chair, and there were other ladies with her, but William hardly noticed them. She was dressed in a crimson velvet petticoat, and a jewelled bodice, and her gown was of white satin, stitched with pearls. A snow-white ruff stood up round her face, and her hair was bound with a headdress of golden wire and rubies. There was a golden collar round her neck, and she wore ruby ear-rings. In one hand she carried a jewelled pomander filled with sweet-smelling spices, and she fanned herself with a silver fan. As William took off his cap and bowed, she said, 'Come here, William, you are welcome. I am sorry that Sir Fulke is not at home, but he will be back soon, and meanwhile you must make do with such poor company as you find here.'

William bowed again. He knew that he should have made some complimentary reply, but he could think of nothing to say. He saw now that there were four ladies with her. One was elderly, and very plainly dressed, two wore fashionable clothes, but without jewels, and the last was a young girl whom he guessed to be Lady Anne's daughter, for she was more richly dressed than the others, and sat on a stool beside Lady Anne.

'Come nearer. Do not be afraid,' said Lady Anne, with a note of boredom in her voice, beginning to fan herself again. 'This is my daughter, Mistress Margaret, and these are my ladies, Mistress Ursula and Mistress Catherine and Mistress Jane. If you are to come and live in my household, you must look upon us all as your friends.'

As William came close, Margaret Greville raised her eyes from the cut-work which she was doing, and enquired, 'Do you think you are going to like us, Master William?'

For a moment, William felt stupid and tongue-tied again. But then, under the fashionable head-dress and the plucked eye-brows, he saw in Mistress Margaret's face exactly that look of mischief which he had so often seen in Joanne's, when she was teasing Rufus.

'Mistress, I will promise to like you twice as well as you like me,' he said.

Lady Anne stopped fanning herself, and looked at her daughter, smiling.

'But supposing we don't like you at all!' cried Mistress Margaret. 'I know arithmetic, you see. Twice nothing is nothing. It will be very rude of you not to like us, just because we don't like you.'

The ladies looked back at William. He felt exactly as though he was playing a game of tennis.

'Oh, but you *must* like me!' he said. 'It's part of the bargain.'

'What? Why, we made no bargain!'

'Yes,' said William. 'You are to like me half as much as I like you – and I like you a great deal already, so you must like me a little.'

'Oh well, if we must, we must!' said Margaret, throwing up her hands, and then all the ladies laughed and Lady Anne said kindly, 'William, we shall like you well. Sir Fulke says that you have a pleasing voice. Will you take the lute and sing to us?'

'Yes, Madam,' answered William.

He felt that he had passed the first test at Beauchamp Court – but that there were many more to come!

*

When Sir Fulke returned, with several other gentlemen, he spoke to William kindly, and said he hoped he would be happy there. He explained to William that on more formal occasions he would be expected to stand behind his chair and serve him, but that this was only a family dinner.

'Only a family dinner!' thought William. 'What *do* they do for banquets?'

A trestle-table had been set up at the foot of the other one for the servants, and William half expected to find himself there, but instead he was at the lower end of the big table, with such people as Master Malet, and the Frenchman who had come to give Mistress Margaret a French lesson, and some of the attendants of Sir Fulke's guests. William found himself next to another page, a fair-haired, blue-eyed boy, a year older than himself, called Michael Drayton.

'There is my master,' said Michael, 'Sir Henry Goodere, sitting next to Lady Anne. He has some business with Sir Fulke about a dispute with another landowner over a land-boundary.'

'Oh,' said William, looking solemn.

Michael laughed.

'There are always disputes over land-boundaries,' he said. 'I sometimes wonder how the gentlemen would occupy their time without them. First they meet together and talk about them, with maps spread out over the study table. Then they go to the place and look at the boundary. and talk to all the local people, and ask the oldest inhabitant where it was in his grandfather's time, and he can't remember, but he pretends he can. And then, if they still can't agree, they take it to law, and they all go up to London, taking the oldest inhabitant with them. Only by then he has usually died, so then they take depositions instead from people who remember what he said, and so it goes on. Oh, it's great fun!'

'If Sir Henry Goodere went to London, would you go with him?' asked William.

'Yes, certainly. And you'd go with your master if he went. How long have you been in Sir Fulke's service?'

'Er – not long,' answered William. Then he smiled and added, 'Since this morning!'

'Oh, you'll like being a page!' cried Michael, earnestly. '*I* do! Sir Henry is the best Master in the world. He is like a father to me, and I should be happy to serve him for the rest of my life.'

William thought to himself that *he* wouldn't be satisfied only to serve Sir Fulke Greville for the rest of *his* life, but he didn't say so.

After dinner, Sir Fulke went into his study with Sir Henry Goodere, and the ladies walked in the garden, inviting William and Michael to join them. William found himself walking with Margaret Greville, amidst hedges of sweetbrier, and treading on paths turfed with sweet herbs.

'My father tells us that you write charming songs, William,' she said, 'and set them to music.'

'Oh, that is only to amuse myself,' William answered.

'And what do you do *not* only to amuse yourself?'

William hesitated, glancing sideways at Mistress Margaret. She was smiling, but very kindly.

'I – write poetry,' he said.

'And do you hope to have your verses printed one day?' she asked.

'I've never thought of it,' said William. 'But I hoped once –'

He stopped. She turned to him, smiling, and put her hand on his arm.

'Tell me what you hoped,' she said.

'I hoped to go to Court one day,' said William, in a low voice, thinking how far away such a hope was now.

Margaret clapped her hands.

'But, of course!' she exclaimed. 'You shall go with my brother Fulke. You know what a favourite he is with the Queen! And he is a poet, too! I daresay my father thought of that when he brought you here. You shall go to London with my brother, and read your poems to the Queen, and have a place at Court!'

'If only I could!' cried William, laughing.

'You must work hard while you are here,' said Mistress Margaret, 'and read all you can – for my brother is a great scholar – and I will ask my mother if you can share my tutors for lessons in French and music. Would you like that?'

'Very much,' said William. 'You are very kind.'

Margaret laughed.

'You won't say that when Monsieur Le Brun is scolding you for not learning your irregular verbs,' she said. 'Heavens! I must go now, or he will scold me for being late for my lesson! Next time he comes, I will ask my mother if you can join us. Oh, we will make you a Court Poet yet!'

She hurried gaily away, leaving William more excited and hopeful than he had been at any time since he first heard that his father had lost his money.

*

The months which followed were anxious and busy but very happy for William. To his relief, Sir Fulke decided that he was not to wear a livery – or rather, he said, 'My Lady did not wish it.' Instead, Master Malet was told to order William two suits of clothes from the tailor, including a velvet cloak and a pair of velvet shoes, so that he no longer clattered about the Gallery in the evenings.

With Sir Fulke he went hunting, learning to know the voices of the hounds, and to name the deer by their antlers. Going hawking, he learnt something of that art, too, and loved to see the falcon tossed into the air like a sky lark, plummeting cruelly down upon its prey, and then returning, at the falconer's call, as gentle as a dove to rest upon his wrist.

As winter came on, braziers were lit in the gallery, and there William would often sit with the ladies, while they did their embroidery, reading to them from the translation of Plutarch's Roman histories, or from the new romance called *Euphues*. Sometimes there would be games, or dancing, and then William often found himself learning the steps from Margaret Greville, for he only knew the old country dances, and she would say, laughing, that he mustn't disgrace them when he came to dance before the Queen in London.

The house was always full of guests, and William several times saw Michael Drayton again. He discovered that Michael, too, wrote poetry, and they would often sit together in the gallery, when their masters were busy in the study, reading from the same book (only William read much faster!) or composing sonnets on the same subjects – only William was quicker at this, too, and would often write two or three while Michael was writing one! A favourite subject with William just now was the beauty of a dark-haired lady, but if he showed his poems to Margaret Greville (whose hair was dark) she would laugh and say that black was an unfashionable colour, and that she thought she would dye her hair red, and that then he would have to re-write all his sonnets.

But all this time, however busy the days were, and however tired he was when he finally drew the curtains on Sir Fulke's great bed and lay wearily down in his own small one in the outer room, William never quite lost the feeling of expectancy which had come to him when Mistress Margaret first spoke of her brother, Fulke Greville.

And at last, in the spring, he heard that young Fulke Greville was coming home.

12

The Poet and his Friend

'William!' shouted Master Malet, in his high, harsh voice, 'William! Where are you?'

'Hush!' said William, staying where he was. 'Not so loud. You know my lady hates loud voices.'

'So she does,' said Master Malet, quite seriously. 'I had forgotten.' And then he went on in a respectful mutter, 'Have you perfumed Master Fulke's room? And Master Philip Sidney's? And did you move the cedar chest into Master Fulke's room? And have you taken Master Fulke's hunting-coat downstairs to be aired?'

'Yes, and yes, and yes,' said William, 'and, no, because I couldn't find it.'

'Oh dear me!' said the steward, starting off along the gallery. 'I shall have to find that coat myself. Although it's so shabby, Master Fulke always wears it for riding when he is at home.'

'Master Malet,' William called after him, 'you have forgotten something.'

He turned back at once.

'No, William, have I?' he said anxiously. 'What is it?'

'I don't know,' William answered gravely. 'But you are sure to have forgotten something.'

'So I am,' said poor Master Malet, setting off again. 'So I am. Now, I must find the hunting-coat first, and then

I must speak to the cook and make sure he remembers that Master Fulke likes oranges with his chicken—'

And away he went. William looked after him quite affectionately. He didn't in the least mind obeying him, as long as he could laugh at him at the same time. And since Master Malet had no sense of humour, he never knew, so they were both happy.

'What a pother everyone is making!' said William. 'I'm sure my parents wouldn't make such a fuss if *I* were coming home.'

'Ah,' said Michael Drayton, who was sitting reading, beside him, 'but then *you* are only William Shakespeare. If you were the great Fulke Greville, that would make a difference.'

'I'm not so sure it would,' said William, laughing. 'I can just hear my mother if she was Lady Anne, instead of plain Mistress Shakespeare: "Well, my boy, there you are! Been presented at Court, have you? Gone on a mission to Europe for the Queen, have you, and met Don John of Austria and the Prince of Orange? A great favourite of the Queen's, are you, and she's so fond of you that she will hardly let you out of her sight? H'm, well, don't let it make you proud!"'

'I'd be proud if I were him,' said Michael. 'Think of it – not yet thirty, and already famous! They say that he and his friend, Philip Sidney, are two of the most admired young men in Europe.'

He and William looked at each other, each wondering what it was like to be famous. There was a burst of laughter from the other end of the gallery, where the gentlemen were rhyming on the ladies' names.

'I loved my love with an "M",' chanted Richard Verney, a young gentleman only a year older than William, who was often at the house.

I loved my love with an 'M',
I love her yet
Because she is not marred,
But Margaret!

The ladies laughed again, and the two pages looked at each other and cast up their eyes. These gentlemen who fancied they could rhyme! Michael returned to his book, but William sat gazing out of the window at the pretty, formal garden, and the green park beyond. He saw himself riding with young Fulke Greville on the road to London. He saw Westminster, and the great houses by the river, and the Queen's Palace of Whitehall. He saw the narrow streets of the city, and saw himself at the play, sitting on the stage, perhaps, fanning himself with a feathered hat, and he saw himself at Court, amidst all the great nobles, and heard Fulke Greville say, 'Your Majesty, here is my friend, William Shakespeare, who would be honoured if he might read you some of his poems.' And then the Queen, stately and wonderful, glittering with jewels, would smile and say—

There was a sudden interruption. Horses' hooves sounded on the pavement, and the heavy door downstairs was dragged open. Master Malet could be heard shouting orders, and servants ran outside with a great bustle and clatter. Amidst all the running to and fro and the thumping of heavy luggage being set down, could be heard Master Malet's flowing speech of welcome, and then footsteps on the stairs. William and Michael put down their books and stood up.

The two young men who came up the stairs were remarkably alike. They were both richly dressed under their travelling cloaks, and both wore tall, plumed hats. They had the same shape of face, with rather long noses, very slightly curved, and small mouths. But one of them had a very gentle, open look, and a smile which seemed to say that he would never willingly hurt anyone but himself, while the other had a small moustache and slightly drooping eyelids, and though he too smiled, it rather seemed to be at others than at himself.

The group at the other end of the gallery fell silent. As William and Michael bowed to the young men, there was a sudden movement and a cry, and Lady Anne came swiftly forward. There was such a light on her face that William thought for a moment that the sun had come out, and glanced at the window, surprised to see that it was the same grey day as before.

'My son!' cried Lady Anne. 'My dear son!'

The slightly taller man, with the moustache, stepped forward, and took off his hat, and she put her arms about him. It was wonderful to see her so happy – and yet William could not help wishing that Fulke Greville had been the other young man, who stood by, smiling so gently.

Fulke Greville knelt down in front of his mother, and she put her hands on his shoulders and said, 'God bless you, my son.' Then, as he stood up, she turned to Philip Sidney and kissed him too.

'Dear Philip, you are very welcome,' she said, 'not only for yourself, and as my son's old schoolfellow, but because I swear this runaway would never come to his home if you didn't sometimes take him by the hand and bring him here with you!'

Philip Sidney smiled. 'If Fulke is often away from home, Madam,' he said, 'you must blame the Queen, who will not part with him, but keeps him at Court with her.'

'Yes, and Her Highness uses strong persuasion,' Fulke added. 'When she sent for me after I had tried to embark for the Netherlands without her permission, I thought she was going to box my ears.'

'As long as she keeps you safely away from the wars,' cried Lady Anne, 'I would not mind if she boxed your ears every day.'

'Oh, Mother, don't say that!' Fulke protested. 'The Queen hits as hard as a man – and twice as unexpectedly.'

Then they all laughed and moved towards the group of ladies and gentlemen at the other end of the gallery, whom the young men greeted with bows and smiles and graceful speeches, and many apologies, too, for coming upon them in all the mud and dirt of their journey.

'That is soon put right!' said Lady Anne. 'William!' she called, 'you shall take Master Fulke to his room, and see that he has all he needs. This is your father's new page, Fulke. His name is William Shakespeare, and he comes from Stratford.'

William bowed, and Lady Anne turned to Philip Sidney, taking him affectionately by the arm.

'I shall do myself the honour of being your attendant for this time,' she said. 'And on the way you shall tell me about Fulke's health, and whether he remembers that he is our only son, and takes good care of himself.'

William noticed that as soon as Master Greville was away from the rest of the company, he became at once silent and grave. In the small corner bedroom, made even smaller by the great bed, but with a fine view over the park towards Alcester, his servant had already carried up his luggage, and was taking out clean shirts and stockings.

'Will you change, sir?' he asked.

'No,' said Fulke, sitting down on the oak joined stool and leaning back against the wall. 'Give me a clean ruff and clean stockings.'

'Shall I pull off your boots, sir?' asked William.

The young man nodded, and William knelt down before him. He was delighted at the chance to be alone with Master Fulke so soon, and, in his mind, he heard all the things he wanted to say. 'Mistress Margaret showed me some of your sonnets, sir,' he would begin. Or, 'I write poetry, too, sir.' Or, perhaps, quite simply, 'Sir, when you go back to London, will you take me with you?' But the boots were off, and he was fetching water and a towel and still he had not spoken. He went on one knee to present the silver bowl of scented water, and then handed Master Fulke a clean towel, glancing timidly up at him. The young man still looked very grave, and there was something in his face which made William feel that it would not be a good idea to speak to him first.

The servant came near with the clean ruff. William stood up, and Master Fulke nodded in dismissal. In another moment William was outside the door, and still Master Fulke had not spoken to him so much as a word. But still, he thought, there would be many more chances.

●

Dinner that day was a formal banquet, and as the courses came and went, beef, mutton, veal, chicken, rabbit, swan, artichokes, sweet potatoes, turnips, and fritters with custard, followed by lamb, pheasant, pigeons, larks, hares, peacock, salads, fish, tarts, and oranges, with wine served in delicate goblets of Venetian glass, the two pages, standing behind their masters' chairs, listened enthralled to the conversation at table. It seemed as though the two young men had been everywhere and known everyone. If they were not talking of the Queen and her nobles, or of their journeys in France and the Low Countries, then it was of Master Fulke's sea-voyage around Ireland, and of the young eagle which he had taken from its nest, high on a rocky crag.

'Oh, Fulke!' cried Lady Anne in horror, 'that was so dangerous!'

But he only laughed, and William, meeting Michael's eye across the table, thought that he would gladly follow such a man across the world, meeting kings and nobles, and performing deeds of daring.

The two boys ate their meal with the servants after the guests had finished, feasting off the many dishes which had been left almost untouched. Afterwards, they made their way up to the gallery. It was like a painted picture there, with the ladies sitting in a circle, their bright skirts spread wide over hooped farthingales, and the gentlemen in their brilliant doublets, with gay hats and jewels in their ears, leaning over them or sitting on the ground beside them. In the centre of the group was Lady Anne, with her son and his old schoolfellow close beside her. As the two pages came near, Margaret Greville smiled at William, drawing her skirt aside so that he could sit down at her feet, and then turned back to the argument which was going on.

'Oh, come!' Richard Verney was saying, 'you will never convince us of that! Why, the whole art of poetry is imitation and invention. And will you tell us that poetry is truer than history?'

He was sitting on the other side of Mistress Margaret, and he played with the chain of the silver comfit-box which hung from her waist, and laughed as he spoke, but Philip Sidney replied quite seriously.

'Indeed, poetry has more truth!' he cried. 'The historian only tells us what happened, but the poet tells us also what *might* happen, and what *should* happen. He is at once historian, philosopher and preacher.'

'Heavens!' exclaimed Richard, still laughing, 'I'd no idea it was such a noble thing to be a poet. The next thing we know, every tradesman in England will be selling his shop and writing verses!'

'Ah, but if it is such a noble thing,' said one of the older ladies, 'why do so many learned men say that poetry is wicked and worthless?'

'It isn't the fault of poetry, but of poets,' said Fulke Greville in his clear, decided voice. 'Poetry should be plain and pithy, and instead they fill their verses with a lot of ridiculous and extravagant fancies.'

William had become so much engrossed in the argument that he had forgotten where he was.

'But surely, sir,' he said, 'fancy is the material a poet works in, just as a painter uses paint. If we write too plainly, what will be the difference between poetry and prose?'

Fulke Greville raised his eyebrows, looking at William from his heavy-lidded eyes, and there was a brief silence.

'*We?*' he said, with a note of sardonic amusement in his voice.

'Hold your tongue, William!' cried Lady Anne. 'Things have come to a pretty pass when a page takes it upon himself to contradict a gentleman! Be silent, sirrah, and speak when you are spoken to!'

So now William knew what Thomas, the servant, had meant when, talking of Lady Anne, he had said, 'Hoo!' There was another silence, in which William wished himself a hundred miles away. Even Margaret Greville was abashed by her mother's anger, and though she murmured 'William writes poetry, too, you see,' it was only under her breath. But softly as she spoke, Philip Sidney heard her.

'I didn't know William was one of us,' he said, smiling.

'Lady Anne, you couldn't expect a poet to keep silent while we debated his art.'

'I expect him to know his place, and not speak when his betters are speaking!' said Lady Anne, and then even Philip Sidney could say no more.

*

For William, there was little pleasure in the young men's visit after that. He spent a great deal of time in their company, hunting and hawking, carrying their rods when they went fishing in the moat or in the stream, fetching books for them, and even singing and playing to them when he was asked. But between him and Fulke Greville there was – not exactly an enmity – but something which made it impossible for them to know and understand each other. It was not that Master Greville was an unpleasant young man. Master Malet and many of the servants loved him dearly, and his graceful manners made him a great favourite with all the ladies. And it wasn't that he thought himself better than anyone else. William thought rather that he seemed to have a contempt for himself, and that this gave him a contempt for everyone else, too. Even when he was at his most gay and charming, laughing and paying elegant compliments to the ladies, William would sometimes see on his face a moment afterwards a look which seemed to say, 'How stupid and ridiculous all this is! Why do I bother with it?'

After that first day, William took great care never to offend him, and sometimes Master Fulke would be so pleasant with him that he began to feel quite easy in his company. Then one day Master Malet gave an order, William answered teasingly, and Master Fulke, nearer at hand than he had thought, said sharply, 'Do not be impertinent, sirrah! Do as you are told!' and William was made to feel once more that his master's son was a great man, and that he himself was nothing. (He never felt this with Philip Sidney, though *his* mother was the daughter of the Duke of Northumberland, and his uncle was the Earl of Leicester.)

On the last afternoon of their stay, most of the guests had left, and the two young men were amusing themselves in the gallery by writing sonnets. William was sent to fetch more paper from the study, and when he returned Fulke was saying, 'Let us both use the same first line as in that poem by Edmund Spenser. Here, I'll copy it out.'

He took the paper from William, and added pleasantly, 'You write verses. Why don't you try your hand at it, too?'

William hesitated, and then fetched a stool and came to join them.

'Here's a pen,' said Fulke without looking up, and Philip Sidney, smiling, pushed his own beautiful silver travelling ink-box towards him.

They all three worked very differently. Fulke Greville wrote with a careless concentration, frequently crossing out and interlining. Philip Sidney seemed to write for pleasure, smiling as he did so, and never putting quite all his mind to it. As for William, he sat gazing out of the window until the whole sonnet was in his mind, and then he wrote it down very quickly and neatly without changing a word. When the two young men had finished, they smiled at each other and exchanged their papers. Philip Sidney took longer in deciphering Greville's, and Fulke idly picked up William's. He raised his eyebrows at it.

'What a neat hand you write!' he said, looking amused. 'You should be an usher in a school!'

He glanced through William's sonnet, still smiling.

'No wonder you defend fancy in a poet!' he said. 'I believe there is an image in nearly every line, and in some there are two! Whatever your handwriting is like, no one will ever complain that you write too plainly, that's certain!'

He tossed the paper down on the table, just as Sir Fulke from downstairs called to them to come and see the horse which he proposed to give his son as a parting present.

'I must see your poem later, William,' said Philip Sidney, as they hastily got up.

'Yes, sir,' said William.

Left alone, he picked up the three poems and read them through. He sat for a long time looking at them. He knew there was not a creature in England who would not think him mad if he said so, and appallingly vain, too, and yet, something too deep for argument, too certain for doubt, told him that of the three poems, his was the best.

*

Before they left next morning, each of the young men gave William a gold coin, and Philip Sidney spoke to him kindly, telling William to let him know if he could ever help him in any way. They took their leave of Lady Anne and Sir Fulke and Mistress Margaret, with Master Fulke once more kneeling for a blessing from his mother and father. Then they had mounted their fine, spirited horses, and went off at a dancing pace down the avenue, followed by their servants and the two rumbling coaches which carried their luggage.

William stood on the steps and watched them go. He could not know that, six years later, Philip Sidney, as famous for gentleness in his death as he had been during his life, would be killed in the fighting near Arnhem. But he knew already that there was little hope of advancement from young Fulke Greville.

13

The Actors Again

After that visit, William was never quite happy at
Beauchamp Court. Sir Fulke was as kind and cheerful
as ever, but Lady Anne, though she wasn't angry with
him again, never seemed now to speak to him as a mem-
ber of the family, but always as Sir Fulke's page.

Something else had happened, too, which made a great
difference to William. Before young Fulke Greville left,
his sister and Richard Verney were betrothed, taking
hands before the assembled company, and making a
solemn promise to marry. William wasn't in love with
Mistress Margaret. Certainly not, he told himself. That
would be ridiculous. But seeing her so busy with her bride-
clothes and wedding-gifts, making plans for the rebuild-
ing of her new house and choosing her coach and horses,
William felt that he had lost a friend and a playfellow.
There were no more shared French or dancing lessons,
and no more pleasant hours spent in showing Mistress
Margaret the fingering of the lute. Somehow, all the
adventure and gaiety had gone out of his life at Beauchamp
Court, and the days went by in work and sameness, with
nothing to look forward to. It was as though he had put his
foot on a stepping-stone, and it had turned into a prison.

When William first left Stratford he had hardly been
homesick at all, and the few times he had gone there with
Sir Fulke, and had called at Henley Street, he had been

rather annoyed to find that his family were still busy with their own affairs, and had only a passing interest in Sir Fulke's new falcon, or in the handsome horse which had been set aside for his own use, or in the rhyming riddle he had made on Mistress Ursula's name, and how the ladies had laughed when they solved it. But now, he was suddenly very glad when Sir Fulke's dispute over land-boundaries in Shottery brought him on frequent journeys to Stratford. Instead of strolling in for a ten minutes' visit and hurrying back to eat at the inn, or with Sir Fulke's friends, he several times asked permission to go home to dinner. And if at first it seemed strange to cut his meat up with his own knife, and eat off wooden or pewter trenchers instead of silver plates, yet, sitting there amongst the family in the clean, bare room, with his father and Gilbert coming in from the shop and his mother and Joanne from the kitchen, somehow he knew that this was really his kind of life, and that it always would be.

He had a new brother now, a beautiful, sturdy little boy, already very spoilt, who refused to be left out of any-thing, and was always scuttling across the room like an energetic crab if he thought they were doing anything which might interest him. He was called Edmund, after their Uncle Edmund Lambert.

'Though we never would have named him that,' said Mary Shakespeare, indignantly, 'if we'd known your uncle would behave so badly.'

'Couldn't Father pay off the mortgage?' asked William.

'Pay it off? Yes!' said his mother. 'He offered your uncle the money to redeem the land, but your uncle refused to take it, saying your father owed him other money as well, and that he'd collect it all together. Now he says your father's broken the agreement to repay the money within the year, and he won't part with the land.'

'When a man's down,' said John Shakespeare gloomily, 'everyone is ready to put a foot on him – even his relations.'

'The land's gone, then,' said William.

'Certainly not!' said his father, cheering up. 'As soon as I can, I shall take your uncle to law for it. Things are a little difficult just at present, but trade is sure to improve soon, and then we'll get the Wilmcote and Snitterfield holdings back – yes, and buy up your uncle's land, too, you'll see!'

It was like old times to William to see his father so cast down one minute, and then, a moment later, making such wonderful plans. But when they were alone, his mother told him that she thought the land was gone for ever, and that his father's business was in such a bad way, she didn't see how it could ever recover.

'And I'm no help,' said William.

'Nonsense!' said his mother. 'The sum of money Sir Fulke gave us when you went into his service paid off some debts and kept your father out of prison. I dare say one of these days Sir Fulke will find a better place for you – as his agent, perhaps, or he might even let you have a farm.'

William thought with a shudder what it would be like if he were tied for the rest of his life to being a tenant farmer – but what else could he do? He sat and looked at his mother as she turned up the hem of one of Richard's shirts ready for Edmund to wear, and things had never looked so black to him, not even when Fang and Snare were at the door.

'Promise me one thing, William,' said his mother, resting her sewing in her lap. 'If ever you make money, buy land with it and houses. My father owned land all his life, and left it to his children when he died. Now it looks as though your father and I will leave our children nothing but debts. If I could see my son a landed gentleman again, I should die happy.'

'I promise, Mother,' William answered, smiling.

But he had little hope that he would ever keep the promise.

*

He had come to Stratford alone on business for Sir Fulke, and he rode back the long way round, through Shottery, as he often did. Anne Hathaway was working in the garden of Hewlands.

'Mind you don't pull the lettuces up instead of the weeds!' he called.

She straightened up and looked at him gravely.

'Oh, I don't have to do that,' she said. 'Little William does it for me.' She turned to look at her small step-brother, squatting on the path, helpfully rootling about with a stick. 'No, no, Willy!' she cried. 'That's a lettuce. Go round to the back yard, there's a good boy, and see if any of the hens have got out again.'

She never seemed to get out of temper with her step-brothers and step-sisters, though William knew that her step-mother was a foolish, idle woman, who left most of the housework and the care of the children to Anne. William got off his horse and stood leaning his elbow on the saddle. He found Anne's company very restful after being with the ladies at Beauchamp Court. With her he never felt that he had to try to be clever or witty. With her, he could be himself.

'How is your father today?' he asked.

'Not very well. As it's such a fine day I wanted him to come and sit outside in the garden for a while, but the Wise Woman came to see him last week, and she said that sunshine would be bad for him, and he must stay indoors.'

'Did he ever find out that you went to the play in Stratford that day?' asked William.

'No,' she answered. 'He never did. Sometimes I felt badly at not telling him, but Bart said if there was no harm in it, better not to worry him – and if there was, it was better he shouldn't know.'

'I don't think there was much harm in it,' said William, smiling.

There was a sudden uproar from the back yard, where six-year-old John Hathaway had taken Willy's stick away from him, and Anne went to settle the quarrel. When she came back, William said, 'A company of actors is coming to Beauchamp Court tomorrow. They're lodging there for the night, and giving a play in the evening.'

'I wish I could see it!' cried Anne.

'I wish you could, too!' said William, thinking what fun they had had before, all jostled together in the inn-yard.

He prepared to mount his horse again.

'Would you – would you like to come in for a cup of ale?' asked Anne.

'No, I'd better be on my way,' answered William. 'Sir Fulke will be expecting me, and there'll be arrangements to be made for the players. But I'll come and tell you about the play.'

She smiled and nodded, and as he rode away she didn't at once go back to her weeding. When he turned round at the corner she was still looking after him, and when he waved she shyly lifted her hand in reply. For no reason that he could think of, William suddenly began to feel happier, and, strangely enough, all the way to Beauchamp Court he found himself thinking not of the actors, but of Anne Hathaway.

*

They knew that the actors had arrived next day when they heard the flourish of trumpets in the yard. To William's surprise, Sir Fulke himself went down to welcome them.

'James Burbadge, my old friend!' he cried. 'I am very glad to see you again! Are you well? And your wife? And your son? Or is it two sons?'

'Two sons, sir,' answered the actor, bowing. 'All well, thank you.'

Sir Fulke went amongst the company, greeting several of them by name, and William was surprised again to see how calmly and courteously the actors replied. His mother certainly could never call *them* 'a parcel of rascally players!' They were respectful to Sir Fulke and seemed grateful for his kindness, and yet there was something about them which seemed to say that they were proud of their fellowship, and of the craft they practised, just as William's father had always been proud of belonging to the Mystery of Glovers.

Dinner was over, but a special meal of ale and cold meats had been set out for the players in the hall. Master Malet had given orders for it, and then hastily retired, as though he was afraid the actors might expect him to wait on them. William, since Sir Fulke had gone back to his study, stayed behind, helping them to slices of beef and pasty, and sending for more ale when it was needed.

'I see that crab-apple steward is still here,' said one of them.

'M'm,' said another, cheerfully spearing a pickled gherkin with the point of his knife. 'He's so sour, I should think he gives himself heartburn. Robert, couldn't you work in a joke about him this evening?'

'Better not,' said James Burbadge, who was a large, red-faced man of about fifty, evidently the leader of the company. 'Sir Fulke might not like it.'

They went on eating for a while in silence, very companionably, and then a thin, white-bearded actor, who had been warmly greeted by Sir Fulke as 'old John Perkin,' said anxiously, 'That young fellow is not here yet. I knew we should not have left him behind.'

The other actors looked at each other, and heaved small, irritable sighs.

'We *had* to leave him behind,' said James Burbadge, 'because the blacksmith couldn't get those swords mended in time, so he had to wait to bring them. It's better than if we'd all waited, and all been late.'

'Yes,' said Robert Wilson, the man who'd talked of the 'crab-apple steward.' 'Then we would have missed this excellent meal. Might I trouble you, my young friend, for another piece of pigeon-pie? Thank you.'

'But supposing he doesn't arrive in time for the performance?' insisted John Perkin, shaking his head over his glass of ale.

'Well, then one of us will have to double his part.'

'But we can't. We are all on in his first scene.'

'So we are!' exclaimed the man who had speared the pickled gherkin (John Laneham, William afterwards discovered). 'That is awkward, certainly.'

Old Perkin nodded, glad to have someone else sharing his anxiety at last.

'No, it'll be all right,' said Robert Wilson, carelessly. 'Willy Johnson can do it. He only has two lines in that scene, and I can take those.'

'And how about in the last act?' said John Perkin. 'He's on in the scene before, and there's not time for him to change.'

'Oh well, Augustine will probably arrive in time for the last act.'

'He'd better arrive in time for the first act!' cried James

Burbadge, suddenly raising his voice and getting redder than ever. 'I'll wring his neck if he doesn't. I never knew such a boy for dawdling. He'd miss his cue on the Day of Judgment through gossiping with his guardian angel.'

The actors grinned at each other, and went on talking about arrangements for the play – whether they would need to move the throne to make room for the fight, and whether they had enough swords, in case Augustine *shouldn't* arrive in time. William listened intently. He was just realizing that the play, which to everyone else was a game and a holiday, to these men was work. He thought of the plays he had acted in at school, and of the masque which he had written to be performed at Beauchamp Court last Christmas, with the ladies and gentlemen all dressing up in rich costumes and reciting his speeches in the hall while musicians played in the gallery. All that seemed rather idle and childish when William looked at these actors sitting round the table, eating and talking in this practical way. He remembered what Philip Sidney and young Fulke Greville had said about the ennobling effect of seeing famous men and brave deeds shown upon the stage, and suddenly he envied these actors who earned their living by playing, and whose business was poetry.

*

There was a great deal to do in getting ready for the performance, and since no message came for him from Sir Fulke, William found himself drawn in to helping with the preparations. The little serving-room at the end of the hall had been turned into a tiring room, where the actors could dress, and William helped to carry the heavy baskets in there, and afterwards to unpack the belts and swords, and to lay out the gold garments and jewels which were all together in another casket. Meanwhile, the actors came and went, sorting out the costumes, and here William noticed again something which surprised him. In spite of the apparent muddle in the baskets, and the seemingly careless way the actors dragged out odd doublets and cloaks and hats, in fact each of them took great pains in getting his own clothes ready to wear, checking that all the points were there, and the fastenings on the cloak and the strings on the ruff. He realized that acting was more than their business. It was their life, and they gave it all their attention.

The space at the end of the hall was cleared and set out for the first scene, with great branched candlesticks each side, ready to be lit. The servants were putting chairs and stools ready for Sir Fulke and Lady Anne and the other guests and members of the family and household, who were to be the audience. William was just thinking that he must go and see if Sir Fulke needed him, when James Burbadge came up to him and said, 'Young sir, have you ever acted in a play?'

'Well – yes,' William answered, startled. 'Once or twice. At school, you know.'

'Would you like to play tonight?'

'Oh no!' said William, laughing. 'I don't know the play.'

'Only a small part,' said James Barbadge.

'But—' William began, puzzled, and the actor broke in, in his irritable roar. 'It's that young fool Augustine! He's not here yet. Why don't *you* play his part? You'd enjoy it. Come, now!'

'But there's not time to learn it,' William protested. 'And I don't know if Sir Fulke—'

'He's engaged us to act a play,' said James Burbadge. 'He'll be annoyed if we can't do it properly. He'd want you to help us. Go on. Ask him. He'll say, yes.'

'Well, I—I don't—' William began very doubtfully, but James Burbadge, who was a large and powerful man, urged him through the door into the hall, smiling like a tiger intent upon its dinner, and saying heartily, 'Ask him!'

A few minutes later, William was returning even more doubtfully. He had told Sir Fulke that the actors had asked him to take a small part, and Sir Fulke laughed and said,

'Bless the boy! You're only young once. Go and enjoy yourself!' which, William felt, was hardly the point.

As he came downstairs, he was preparing various escapes, such as, 'I really don't feel there is time for me to learn a part,' or, 'There may not be clothes to fit me,' or even just, 'Why don't you double the part?' But as soon as James Burbadge saw him, he said, 'Ah, there you are. Now, here's your part, with the cues. You see, it's quite short.'

He gave William a small roll of paper, and then took him by the arm and led him, very unwilling, to where a board hung on a nail in the door. 'And there's the plot,' he said. 'Study that, and you can't go wrong. Anyway, there's always the prompter. The boy will show you your costume.' And with that he went off.

William looked at his part. It was certainly short—only a few speeches with two or three words of the actor who was speaking before, all pasted together in a roll. But how on earth could he tell when to go on the stage? He looked at the board, and found that it did give some sort of idea of what went on. 'Enter Sebastien. To him, Caterina. Flourish of trumpets. Enter the Court. Exit Sebastien.' William's part was Rodrigo. As long as he watched for 'Enter Rodrigo,' and then waited for his cue, he would be all right—except that he had no idea how long all the speeches were between the various 'Enters' and 'Exits,' or, indeed, what the play was about.

'Here are your clothes, sir,' said one of the boy-players, and William was grateful for the 'Sir,' as a tribute to his velvet suit. He thought that, after all, if he *did* make a series of terrible mistakes, it was entirely their fault for asking him, instead of making sure that Augustine arrived in time. He wondered if Augustine was the dawdling boy at Stratford who had played the Queen, and felt sure he was.

*

If it *was* the same Augustine, he certainly hadn't grown very much. William, who was broad-shouldered and a good height, found that none of the clothes would fit him, and he decided in the end to make do with his own, adding to them a satin cloak and a rather fine hat. Then he settled down with his hands over his ears to learn his lines.

By the time William decided that he knew the part—and he was thankful that he had always been quick at learning—the ladies and gentlemen were coming down to the hall, laughing and talking, to take their seats for the play. William, breathless with anxiety, muttering his lines, and the cues, and even what he could remember of the plot, watched them with envy, thinking that, but for that young fool, Augustine, he could have been sitting amongst them, idle and carefree.

'All right?' said James Burbadge, looking perfectly magnificent in full armour, with a great plumed helmet. 'Watch the prompter, and you can't go wrong.'

He nodded a signal, and the company's musicians struck up on the edge of the cleared space which was their stage. Then, when everyone was settled, a silence fell, and after that came the familiar sound of the trumpets crying three times that the play was about to begin. Now for the first time William heard it from amongst the players.

Robert Wilson strolled out, to give what was, though William could hardly appreciate it, a very gay and witty prologue. The audience laughed, and several of the actors, waiting to go on, nodded to each other and exchanged a few words and smiled. William, his hands icy cold and trembling, watched the play almost without seeing it. The actors came and went, the prompter on his stool followed the words in his book, and the moment when William must step out on the stage raced towards him like some fearful leap over a precipice. Surely when the moment came, his courage would fail him and he would be unable to move!

The scene began in which William must appear. One of the actors, before going on, touched William on the shoulder and said, 'All ready?' He heard the name, 'Rodrigo,' mentioned, and then heard his cue, and saw the prompter nod at him. Hardly knowing what he was doing, he stepped forward on to the stage.

And immediately everything was changed. It was as though he had just climbed a long, steep hill in mist and confusion, and now stepped out on to a sparkling headland. He saw everything very clearly. His own voice had a quality he had never heard in it before, and the stage seemed to spring beneath his feet like mossy turf, so that he moved lightly and gaily, and all his body had a kind of magic running through it. Somehow he found that he had, without knowing it, followed the course of the play, so that he knew now what part Rodrigo played in it, and did not only speak the lines, but felt what Rodrigo would feel and in some mysterious way invited the audience to feel it too. When he felt them responding to it, he had such a feeling of power that it seemed as though he could never fail at anything again, that as long as he lived, he must always be successful.

William could not help being delighted at the applause which followed him when he left the stage, even though he knew that it was mostly because he was Sir Fulke's page, but it was even better to have the actors come and pat him on the shoulder, or nod and smile at him. It was strange, though, he thought, that James Burbadge said nothing at all, but, as he stood near him for a few minutes, looked at him gravely and in silence.

His first anxiety over, there was time now for William, as he waited to go on again, to enjoy the play, which was a comedy.

'Who wrote it?' he asked John Laneham, as they were both smiling at one of the jokes, and Laneham replied casually, 'Oh, it's one of Robert Wilson's.'

William looked at him in amazement. He had always thought that plays were written by scholars at the universities, or by young noblemen at Court. He had never thought that a man could be an actor and also write plays.

William had been looking over his part in the last act, and he noticed that there was one line in it which was obviously written to be spoken by an actor who was slender and fair-haired – whereas he himself was not. So when he next found Robert Wilson near, he asked if he should change the line a little, to make it fit.

'Do what you like, my boy,' said Robert Wilson, cheerfully. 'Say what you like. The others all do!' and with a glare at the prompter – who obviously took it as a personal insult, and glared back – he strode on to the stage.

In fact, William cut the line out altogether, and said something quite different, which, to his delight, was greeted with a great laugh by the audience.

'That's a good line of yours,' said Robert Wilson, when the play was over and they had all made their bows and were returning to change. 'We'll keep that in.' And William stood looking after him in astonishment, thinking that, wherever the company acted the play, all over the country, in London, or even before the Queen, that line of his would be spoken, and people would laugh at it.

14

The Hired Man

By the time the company had changed, and packed away their clothes and cleared the stage, the family and guests had gone up to the dining-parlour off the gallery for supper, and the servants were setting out the supper tables for the actors and themselves in the hall.

William, pleasantly tired, but still excited, sat down with the company. There seemed to be plenty to talk about – the mistake which someone had made in the second scene, the line which one actor had forgotten and another had managed to say for him, the joke which the audience had laughed at too soon – and the one they had missed altogether. William, sitting in the midst of the actors, had the strangest feeling, as though after many years he had come home, as though these players, whom he had never known before this day, were members of a family to which he, too, belonged, were dear to him, and known to him, and were his own people.

They were half-way through the meal when Augustine arrived, very much aggrieved because he had been given a lift in a farmer's cart, and had discovered much too late that it was going in quite the wrong direction, and been set down miles away to make his way on foot, lugging the heavy sword-bag with him.

'We didn't miss you,' said James Burbadge, and then

Augustine stopped looking aggrieved and looked indignant instead. He was the same boy that William and Rufus had talked to at Stratford, only a little taller, and still very slender, which was surprising, William thought, considering the size of the supper he managed to eat.

Sir Fulke and Lady Anne came down in the middle of the meal, to give, as Sir Fulke said, 'good cheer' to the players, and to thank them for the play and bid them welcome again. Sir Fulke, too, praised William's performance in the play.

'Before we know where we are,' he said, laughing, 'you will be asking William to join you, and making him a sharer in the company!'

'Do you need me now, sir?' asked William.

'No, no,' answered Sir Fulke, kindly. 'You stay and finish your meal. If I need you, I will send for you.'

When Sir Fulke and Lady Anne had returned upstairs, and the players were taking their seats again, James Burbadge looked across at William and said, 'Well?'

' "Well?" ' repeated William, bewildered.

'Would you like to join the company?' said James Burbadge.

William would have thought that he was joking, except that he looked perfectly serious, and even, as he drank his ale and set the cup down with a thump, a little surly.

'But I don't – I don't know anything about—' William began.

'I'd take you as a hired man,' said James Burbadge. 'Pay you a small wage, and teach you the trade. You should make a good actor, and— Can you write? Poetry, I mean, that sort of thing?'

'Yes,' said William.

'That's what I thought. You could do some play-mending. We're always needing that. Work hard, save your money, and you might buy a share in a company one day. Well? What about it?'

'I don't know,' said William, still bewildered. 'I'd like to, but – there's Sir Fulke—'

'Are you bound to him?'

'No. Only for a year, and that's over. Now I serve him for wages.'

'He'd let you go if you asked him, then.'

'Yes,' said William. 'Yes, I suppose he would. But there's my parents. What would my father say?'

He said his father, but he was really thinking of his mother, who had always had such a poor opinion of actors and would think it such a wild and irreligious life.

James Burbadge looked at him in silence for a few moments, and when he spoke again he didn't look like a slightly blustering, irritable actor, but like a very reliable man, of good sense and kindness.

'See here, my boy,' he said. 'I know what people say about actors, and very often they're right. But this is a good company, with a noble patron, and a warrant for playing from the Queen herself. Here it is. You can see it. I've got two boys of my own, and I'm breeding one of them up to follow a trade in the Theatre. I wouldn't do that, believe me, if I was ashamed of it. There are honest men who are actors, and honest men who aren't. If you're an honest man yourself, and follow your calling as an honest man should, your parents will live to be proud of you, whether you're a shoemaker or a player – or a joiner, which I was once. Come, now, will you profess the quality of acting? I swear you won't regret it.'

'I'd like to join you,' said William, 'but—'

'Right!' said James Burbadge. He thumped the table. 'Bring ink and paper!' he shouted. 'Oh, devil take it! I was thinking we were in a tavern! Augustine, make your-self useful. Fetch my bag from the tiring room.'

'Yes, but—' William protested.

'We'll sign an agreement now,' said James Burbadge. 'Much the best thing. Then we both know where we stand.'

'But, I can't!' cried William. 'I must ask Sir Fulke first, and my father—'

'Where does your father live?'

'In Stratford.'

'H'm. And we move on early tomorrow.'

William gazed at him in dismay. The whole glorious adventure seemed to be slipping through his fingers. But his mother and father came first. The duty and affection which he owed to them was a debt which must be paid, and he could not forget it, even for the promise of a whole world of glory and excitement.

Augustine banged the bag down on the table, and winked disrespectfully at William over James Burbadge's head, but William was too much beset by anxiety and regret to wink back. James Burbadge slowly got out paper and ink, and set it out on the table, pushing the dishes aside.

'Can you make your way to London,' he asked, 'if they agree?'

'Yes, sir.'

'Very well, then. Here's what we'll do. We'll make out an agreement, sign it, and have it witnessed. If you can come, bring it with you, and put it into my hands. If you can't, burn it. Agreed?'

'Oh yes, sir!' cried William.

James Burbadge sniffed, wiped his nose on the back of his hand, cleared the table a bit more, and then settled down to write in a crabbed, unscholarly hand.

'Mem,' he wrote, 'That the 24th August 1581, I hired Wm. Shakespeare with 2 pence, to serve two years in the quality of playing for 5s. a week for one year and 6s. 8d. a week for the other year which he hath covenanted himself to serve me, and not to depart from my company till this 2 years be ended. Witness to this.'

Then he signed his name, gave the pen to William to sign his, and called, 'Robert, John, Willy, come and witness this, will you?'

The three actors signed their names, and then James Burbadge gave the piece of paper to William.

'Here you are,' he said. 'And here's two pence. Now I've hired you. Bring that paper to me in London at the Theatre in Shoreditch. We shall be back there in a month's time.'

'But supposing I can't come, sir,' said William. 'How about the two pence?'

James Burbadge looked at him, and then suddenly he laughed a great laugh.

'That's the first actor who ever troubled his head about *his* debts to me!' he said. He got to his feet, and patted William on the shoulder. 'If I don't see you again,' he said, 'take it as payment for playing this evening. But I hope I shall see you in September, and for many a long day after that. Tell your father we've a promise that we shall play before the Queen at Christmastide. Tell him, if he's a mind to have a famous son, this is his chance. Come, lads, off to bed. We've an early start tomorrow.'

By the time William had helped to see the players to their beds, the household was quiet. He found that Sir Fulke had gone to bed, without troubling him for his usual duties, and this made him feel that his feet were already set upon this new, strange path. He lay awake for a long time, and thought about it. It was not the laughter or applause which led him now to wish to be an actor, nor even the chance – so astonishingly real at last – of playing before the Queen. He knew that there was much to be suffered in the years to come, many disappointments and uncertainties and humiliations. He knew that to go to London as a common player was a very different thing from going there as a poet, and that London itself, with its brawls and taverns and wickedness, was as dangerous a place as that high crag which Fulke Greville had climbed to take the eagle from its nest. He knew that it depended entirely upon himself whether he plucked from the nest of London that eagle, Fame, or whether he was dashed to pieces on the rocks below. But come what might, he had set not only his hand, but also his heart to professing the quality of playing, and from this day forward he knew that he must be, not only William Shakespeare, poet, but also, William Shakespeare, actor, and maker of plays.

15

The Road to London

One thing William had learnt about his mother was that you never could be sure what she would say, and that the more confidently you expected her to say one thing, the more certain she was to say something quite different. He told his mother and father all about the company, and about James Burbadge, and the warrant from the Queen which actually mentioned the leading actors by name, calling them 'her loving subjects,' and commanding that they should be allowed to play 'without hindrance or molestation' within the City of London and 'throughout our Realm of England.' He showed them the agreement, and explained the terms and the wages, and he mentioned, too, rather casually, as though it was only to be expected, the possibility of playing at Court that Christmas.

When he had finished, there was a long silence. At last, his father said, 'Is this what you really want, William? Never to learn a trade? Never to call yourself a master of your craft?'

'Acting is a craft, Father, of a kind, and James Burbadge is willing to teach it to me. And it's not only the acting. I may write plays as well. And in London I might find a patron for my poetry.'

'Ah,' said John Shakespeare, who in his own affairs had always been so hopeful, 'that's as may be, in the future. But the fact remains that you are proposing to go to

London now as a common player. That isn't what we
hoped for you.'

'What we hoped for William has gone long since,' said
his mother, briskly. 'If this is what he wants to do, he'd
better do it.'

'You mean—' said William, astonished. 'You mean, you
wouldn't mind? You mean, I can go?'

His mother looked at him, and William saw that old
gleam of amusement in the hazel eyes.

'Supposing we said you couldn't?' she enquired. 'What
then? I dare say you'll get into no more mischief in London
than you would if you were eating your heart out in Warwickshire. Besides, you always enjoyed showing off. If
now you've found a way of making money at it, so much
the better.'

'Oh, Mother!' cried William, glowing with pleasure.
'Thank you!'

He looked at his father. John Shakespeare shook his
head, and then slowly smiled.

'Well, Will,' he said, 'you see how it is. Your mother has
made up her mind that you shall go, and so I certainly
can't stop you. Bless you, my son. I hope you become rich
and successful, and excellent in the quality you profess.'

'Thank you, Father,' said William, very gravely, for his
father's blessing was not a thing to be taken lightly. And
then he added, by way of comfort, 'James Burbadge said
that I should make a very good actor.'

'Yes,' said his mother, 'I dare say you may. But don't let
it make you proud.'

On the day William was to leave Beauchamp Court, Sir
Fulke, cheerful and good-humoured as ever, gave William
a purse of money, and gave him also letters of recom-
mendation to several friends of his, in case he should ever
wish to enter their service. William was grateful for the

money, but even more so for the letters, which made him feel that it was not quite such a sink or swim affair after all. There were rafts he could climb on to if necessary – and one of the letters was to Philip Sidney's sister, the Countess of Pembroke, which was a very handsome raft indeed!

Riding alone back to Stratford (he was to leave the horse at an inn for one of Sir Fulke's servants to collect next day) William went by way of Shottery to say goodbye to Anne Hathaway. He had not seen her since the actors came, though he had often found himself thinking of her, and wishing that the distance between London and Shottery was a good deal less than it was.

As he rode up to the house, he saw Anne talking in the doorway to two men, one of them a young Shottery farmer whom William had met a few times with Bartholomew. They went inside as William opened the gate, and Anne turned and saw him and came towards him, smiling.

'Wasn't that Fulke Sandells?' asked William.

'Yes,' Anne answered, 'and John Richardson. They came to see my father. The others are out helping the men with the harvest, but he's not so well today, and I stayed in case he should want for anything. Fulke was telling me, it seems there may be a Chancery suit over that land dispute, and some Shottery folks might have to go up to London to give evidence. Only, now my father's taken to his bed, it doesn't look as if he'll be able to go.'

'That's a pity,' said William. 'I might have seen him there.'

Anne was just leading the way into the parlour. She stopped short, and turned, looking up at William.

'In London?' she said.

'I've joined a company of players,' said William. 'I'm going up to London in a few days' time.'

'Then I shan't see you again !' cried Anne.

William thought that it was so like Anne that she never exclaimed, like everyone else, at the idea of him becoming an actor, but only at the thought that he was going away.

'I shall be back soon,' he answered. 'I promised my mother that whatever happened I'd come back for a visit in a year from now. There's always time between playing, and it's only a three days' journey from London.'

Anne went into the parlour, where the spinning-wheel which she had left when she went to answer the door still stirred silently by the window. She said, without looking at William, 'Ah, you say that now. But when you get to London you'll forget all about us here.'

'Do you think I should forget you?' said William.

She looked up at him then, and smiled.

'Yes,' she replied. 'I do. I think that when you see the London ladies, in all their silks and satins, and jewels on their fingers, we shall look very homespun to you, down here in Warwickshire, and you'll soon forget us.'

'I never shall !' cried William.

She only smiled again, and moved towards the door.

'Have a cup of ale before you go, anyway,' she said. 'I brewed it myself.'

'No, Anne, wait !' cried William, taking hold of her arm. He suddenly knew what he had come to say to her, and that it was more than just, 'goodbye.' She looked up at him, surprised. 'Anne, I haven't any money now,' he said, 'and my father is still in debt. But if I work hard, and find a patron, perhaps, for my poetry, then I shall prosper in London. If I came back a rich man, would you marry me?'

'If I loved you,' said Anne, still smiling, 'I wouldn't want to wait until you were rich. Besides, my father always said he'd settle money on me when I married.'

'Then, if I come back in a year's time—'

'Ah, *if* you do!' said Anne, and started for the door again.

'Don't go!' said William. 'How can I make you believe me? Anne, will you be betrothed to me?'

'What?' said Anne, 'and you going away in a few days? How shall we find time for that?'

William took her hand.

'Now,' he said. 'Here, and now. Will you say you'll marry me?'

'What about my father's permission?'

'I've no money,' said William, 'and he doesn't approve of players. He'd never give his consent. But if we were betrothed – Anne, say now, holding my hand, that you will marry me.'

Anne laughed.

'Well, there are no witnesses,' she said, 'so it wouldn't be a proper betrothal. I suppose there's no harm in it.'

At that moment they heard footsteps on the bare boards overhead, and voices, and then the sound of the two men coming down the stairs. Anne tried to draw her hand away, but William held it tight. He called out, 'Fulke Sandells! Master Richardson! Will you come in here?'

'Will, let me go!' whispered Anne.

'I never will,' said William.

She was suddenly not laughing any more. Fulke Sandells came to the doorway of the room, with John Richardson behind him, and William said in a loud, clear voice, 'I, William Shakespeare, take thee, Anne Hathaway, to be my lawful wedded wife.'

The two countrymen stood there astonished, still in their working clothes, while the bees hummed in the lavender outside the window, and the children's voices came shrill from the harvest field. Anne, her hand in

William's, kept her head bent down, and there was a long silence. Then she looked up at him, and smiled slowly, with tears in her eyes.

'I, Anne Hathaway,' she said, 'take thee, William Shakespeare, to be my lawful wedded husband.'

So Anne and William were betrothed, and four days later he rode away to London.

*

'Is there much danger of thieves on the road?' asked Mary Shakespeare, earnestly. 'And the inns? Are they clean? Are the innkeepers honest? Will the horse be safe in the inn stables? For it is only hired, you know, and has to be returned later by the Carrier.'

'Yes, yes, Mistress,' replied one of William's fellow-travellers, who would much rather have been attending to the loading of his own horse. 'Our English inns are the cleanest in Europe, and the most honest. As for footpads, they won't trouble *us*. We are too well armed for that.'

'I am very glad my son is travelling in such good company,' said his mother. 'I suppose the Carrier knows the road, and you, too, I dare say.'

'Yes, Mistress, I travel up and down—Boy! Pull that tighter! I travel up and down several times a year, and—Boy! Mind what you are about! That cloak-bag is loose!'

The entire Shakespeare family was assembled in the inn yard to see William set off. His father was talking about the price of wool with the Carrier, with whom they were to travel. Richard, dodging round the horses' hooves, appeared to be in far more immediate danger than any of the travellers, and Edmund, bobbing in his mother's arms, reached out his hands towards the horses, saying, 'Ed come too' at intervals. Gilbert leaned against a convenient doorpost and watched the whole scene with silent amusement.

'If you can survive the footpads,' said Joanne, 'and the dirt in the inns, and the dishonest landlords, and can get your horse back after it's stolen, and can find your way to London, I dare say you will do quite well.'

William laughed.

'I hope so,' he said, 'for there's no turning back now.'

They looked at each other soberly for a moment, and William thought how pretty she looked, and how grown-up, although she was only twelve. He said suddenly, 'I wish I could travel by way of Nottingham, and see Rufus.'

'He'll come back to Stratford one day,' said Joanne.

'Do you think he will?' asked William, smiling.

But Joanne replied quite seriously, 'I know he will,' and somehow William felt that she was right, and that William Hart would come back to Stratford one day, and that Joanne would marry no one else until he came.

'Come, young sir, are you ready?' cried the impatient traveller. 'Carrier! Are we ready?'

William could hardly believe that it was really time to go, and he knew from the look on his mother's face that she could hardly believe it either. But in another moment, he had kissed them all goodbye, and had mounted his horse. The other travellers were already clip-clopping after the Carrier out of the inn yard, when William remembered Gilbert and would have turned back, but found him close by his stirrup.

'Gilbert!' called William, suddenly thinking of all the troubles that might come upon the family when he, the eldest son, was far away. 'Gilbert—?'

'Don't worry,' said Gilbert, smiling his quiet smile. 'I shall be here.'

Then William's horse was jerking its head to follow the others, and he found himself in the street. His family came out to see him go, and before he turned the corner into Bridge Street, he looked back and saw them there, his mother and father, Gilbert, Joanne and Richard, and little Edmund crying and reaching out his hands to follow him. William's horse turned the corner, and they were gone.

For a few moments, his eyes were so full of tears that he could see nothing, and blindly sat his horse as it followed the others over Clopton Bridge. But as they turned into the open road, he looked back, and saw the town of Stratford set sturdily on the river-side, and thought of his family, so faithful and so unchanging. And suddenly he knew that what he was doing was right, and that because of them he had the courage for it. Across the fields, in Shottery, was Anne, who had promised to tell her father of their betrothal, and to gain his consent to it, and William knew that no matter when or how he returned, she would be waiting for him. As the horse shook its head and stepped out bravely in the fresh, country air, it seemed to William as though it had always been meant that he should travel to London at last, not with fellow-scholars from the university, or in the train of some rich noble, but undertaking by himself this solitary adventure, and that it was better that it should be so.

He could not know that, after some years of struggle and difficulty, he would become a sharer, with James Burbadge's sons, in the most prosperous company in London, or that he would be known, even in his own lifetime, as the most famous and popular poet and playwright in England. He could not know that his plays would be acted many times before the Queen, or that he would walk with his fellows in a red livery at the Coronation of King James the First. He could not know that, married to Anne, and returning always to Stratford as to his home, he would keep his promise to his mother, and buy a large house there, as well as other cottages, and a piece of land up on Welcombe where once he had sat and dreamed of fame, or that he would one day write 'gentleman' after his name, as his father had wished. Certainly he could not know that four hundred years later his name would be known all over the world, and that his plays would still be acted, and still be loved.

But yet, even then, young, unknown, and almost penniless, he knew what it was that burnt like a proud fire in his heart, and that the poetry which he wrote would live longer than he lived himself. Beneath trees turning from green to gold, and among fields rich with ungathered harvest, young William Shakespeare rode on to fame, and fortune, and immortality.

Letter to the Reader

My dear Reader,

If you have read as far as this (skipping occasionally, I dare say, as I usually do) you may feel that you have done about enough. Still, this letter is for those of you who like to have everything absolutely clear.

Most of the books you read are either fact or invention, and you know quite well which is which. But this story has been a mixture. It had to be.

The 'facts' in the book are that William Shakespeare was born in Stratford-upon-Avon in 1564, and that he had three brothers and two sisters, of whom one sister died young. Everything about his mother and father is true, and the kind of place Stratford was, and the position his father held, and what William would have learnt at the Grammar School, to which, of course, as the bailiff's son, he would have gone. We know that he didn't go to the university, and that his father's money-troubles came at exactly the time when we might have expected him to go. (Another poet, Christopher Marlowe, went to Cambridge on a scholarship, and his father was a shoemaker.) We know that some time between leaving school and being first spoken of as an established playwright, in 1592, William Shakespeare went to London and joined a company of actors. But we don't know when he went, or what he was doing first.

One certain thing is that, even in his early plays like the comedy, *Love's Labours Lost,* he seems to be very familiar with the elegant manners and the witty, poetic talk of Elizabethan ladies and gentlemen. Perhaps he just 'picked it up,' as writers do, from books and from his own imagination, or, as a young actor, from the gentlemen who came to see the plays. Or perhaps, like a poet friend of his, Michael Drayton, he spent a year or two as page in a big household, and read all the books in the library, and ran errands for his master, and wrote his letters, and went hunting with him, and joined in the frivolous or philosophical talk at table or among the ladies in the garden. It's as likely as anything else, and makes more sense than most other guesses. Anyway, in *my* story, that's what happened, and I chose the household of Sir Fulke Greville, whose son was a poet and a friend of poets, and whose house wasn't far from Stratford.

Another of the 'facts' is that our William remained all his life very faithful to his home and his family. He married Anne Hathaway, the daughter of a highly respected farmer in Shottery, and when he made money in London with his plays and the company in which he became a sharer, he invested nearly all of it in land and houses in Stratford, including a fine large house called New Place, in Chapel Street. His sister, Joanne Hart, and her sons were all mentioned in his will when he died. (His three brothers died before he did – young Edmund as an actor in London.)

So you can see how mixed up fact and fancy are in this book, and that it *had* to be. I can't say about it all for certain, 'This is what happened.' But I can say, 'This might well be what happened,' and I've done my best to be able to say, 'There's nothing in this book which *couldn't* have happened.'

Anyway, if it was a good story, I dare say you don't mind, and if it wasn't, you'll mind even less, so I'm pretty safe either way. Goodbye.

Among the books I have consulted are:

William Shakespeare, E. K. Chambers (Oxford University Press).

The Elizabethan Stage, E. K. Chambers (Oxford University Press).

Shakespeare's England (Oxford University Press).

The Elizabethans at Home, Elizabeth Burton and Felix Kelly (Secker & Warburg).

Shakespeare, F. E. Halliday (Thames & Hudson).

The Elizabethan Home, M. St Clare Byrne (Methuen).

Poems and Dramas of Fulke Greville, ed. Geoffrey Bullough (Oliver & Boyd).

My thanks are due to my father, Professor C. J. Sisson, for a great deal of advice and verification, and to Mr Philip Styles, Reader in History at the University of Birmingham, for information about Beauchamp Court.

WITHDRAWN

PR 6069 .I7 1959

Sisson, Rosemary Anne

The young Shakespeare

ustrated by Denise Brown.
9₁

88

OF OHIO

70

SEO Library Center
State Library of Ohio

40780 Marietta Road, Caldwell, OH 43724

1.   I. Title.

PR   60–6950